アシュリー
～All About Ashley～

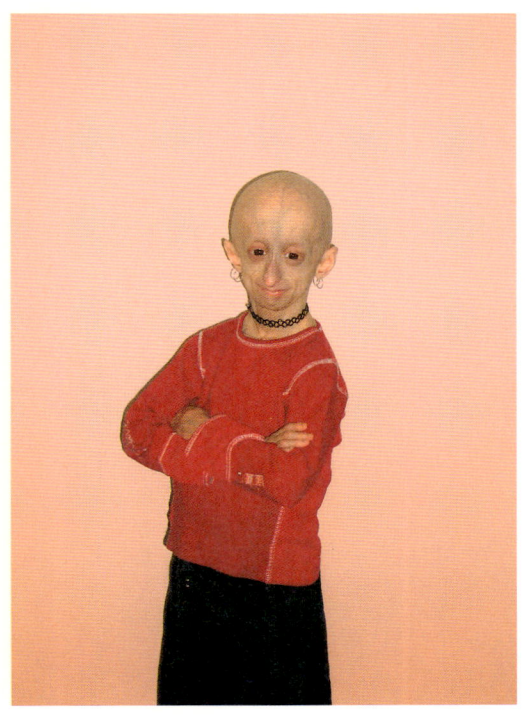

アシュリー・ヘギ 著
Ashley Hegi

アシュリー
～All About Ashley～

目次
◆
Contents

Chapter 1	◆	わたしはアシュリー	◆	I'm Ashley	007
Chapter 2	◆	自分のこと	◆	About Me	019
Chapter 3	◆	わたしの家族	◆	Family	041
Chapter 4	◆	わたしの一日	◆	Daily Life	061
Chapter 5	◆	お気に入り	◆	Favorite Things	073
Chapter 6	◆	学校	◆	School	091
Chapter 7	◆	親友	◆	Best Friend	103
Chapter 8	◆	命	◆	Life	117
Chapter 9	◆	祈り	◆	Prayers	125
Chapter 10	◆	夢	◆	Dreams	135
Chapter 11	◆	ありがとう	◆	Thank You	151

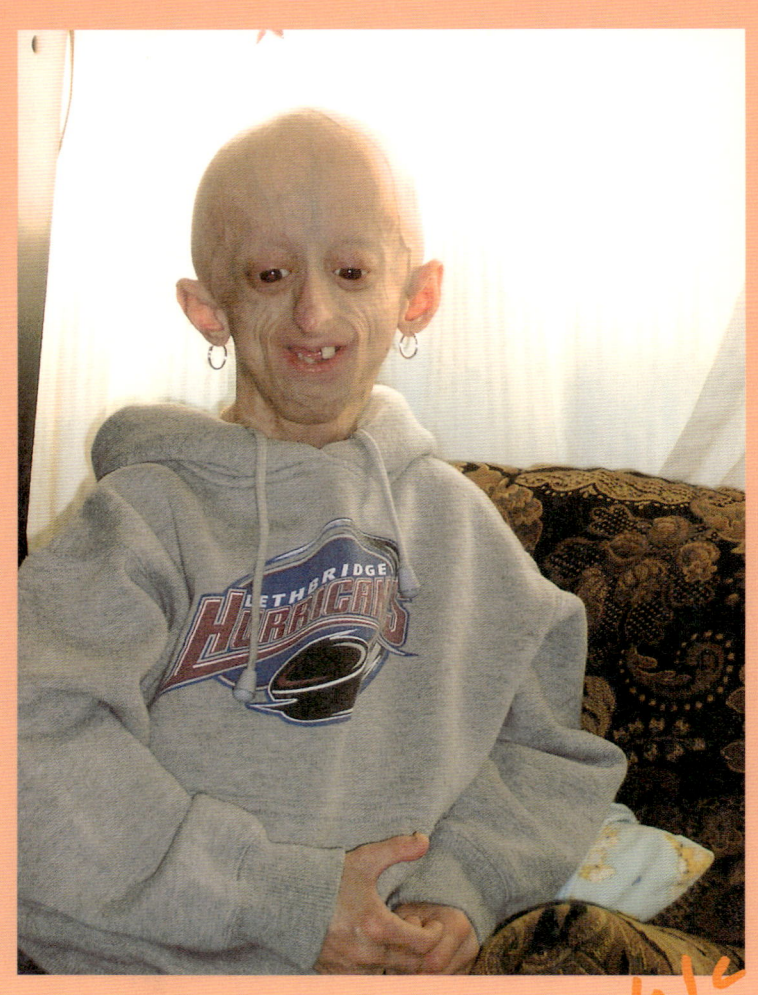

Ashley

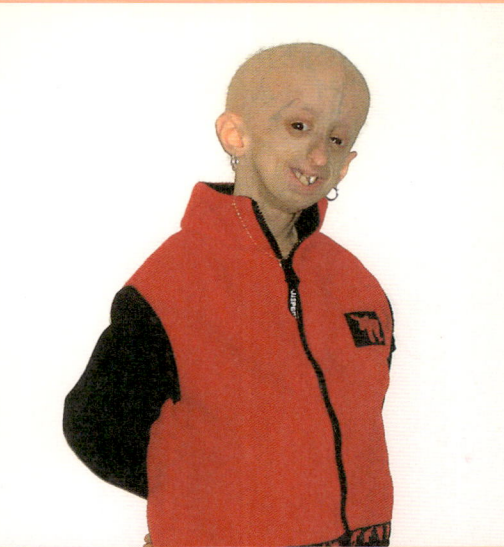

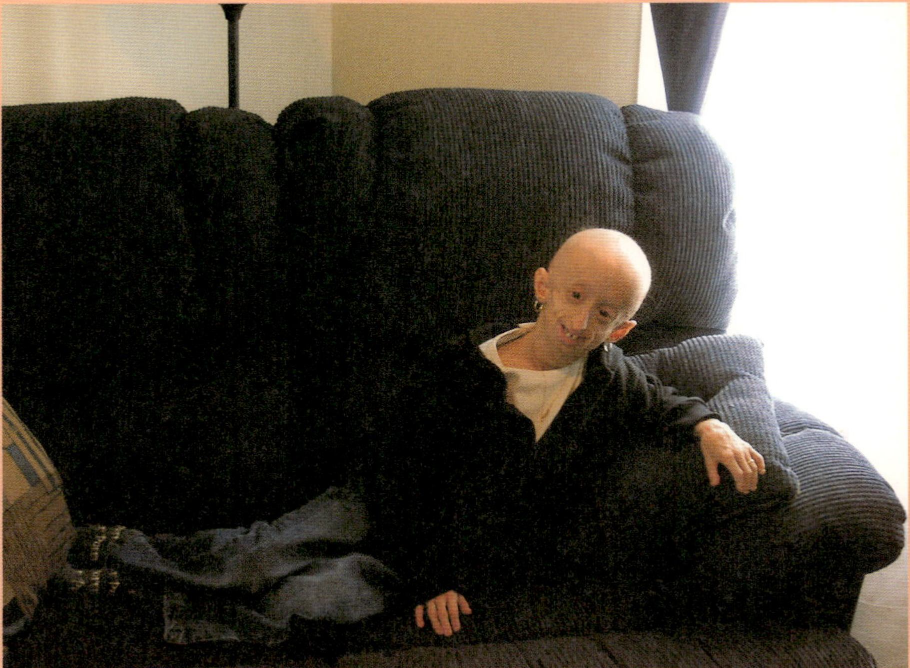

Chapter 1

◆

わたしはアシュリー

◆

I'm Ashley

わたしはプロジェリア。

これは、早く年をとるという、生まれつきの病気。

わたしの体のなかにある時計が、

ほかの人より10倍くらい速く進んでしまうの。

プロジェリアだと、髪の毛が抜けてしまったり、

骨がもろかったりするけど、人にはうつらない。

ただの病気なの。

I have Progeria.
Progeria is a rapid aging disease.
I was born with it.
The clock inside me works about ten times faster than other people.
I lost my hair. My bones are fragile.
But it's not contagious or anything.
It's just a disease.

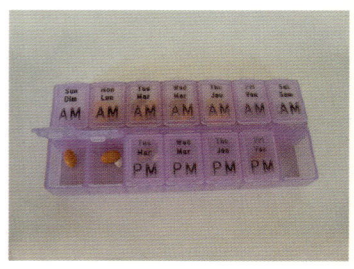

わたしの頭には血管が見えているけれど、

それは、プロジェリアという病気をもっていて、

髪の毛がないからなの。

それ以外は、わたしは何もあなたたちと変わらないの。

You can see veins on my head but it's just because I lost my hair.
Besides that, I am the same as everyone else.

いま14歳。
誕生日は1991年5月23日。
なぜだか誕生日がウイークエンドにあたることが多くて、
うれしいのよね。

自分がプロジェリアだって知って
ショックを受けた、なんて記憶はないの。
だって、わたしは物心ついたときから、
ずっとプロジェリアだったんだもの。

わたしはプロジェリア──ただ、そういうことなの。
そんなの、どうでもいいことだから、
いちいち考えないようにしているわ。

I'm 14 years old.
My birthday is May 23, 1991.
Somehow my birthday is always on the weekend.
I like that.

I don't have any memories of being shocked to know that I had Progeria.
Because, I have had it ever since I can remember.

Although I have Progeria, it's not that big a deal. So I don't think about it.

「おい見てみろよ。エイリアンがいる」って言われたり、
ジロジロ見られたりすることはあるけど、
わたしは、そんなこと気にしないわ。

だって、彼らがわたしをからかおうと思って
やっているんじゃないことはわかってるもの。
彼らは、プロジェリアという病気を知らないだけなの。

彼らはわたしが誰か知らないし、
プロジェリアが何かも知らない。
でも、それは彼らのせいじゃない。
そんなの、みんなが知っているわけじゃないもの。

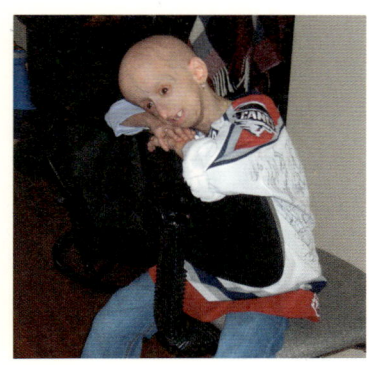

Sometimes people stare at me.
Sometimes kids say to me, " Look, there's an alien! " or whatever,
but I don't really care about them.

Because I know they are not trying to tease me.
They just don't know about Progeria.
They just don't know me.
It's not their fault.
Not a lot of people know about Progeria.

小さいときからよくからかわれたし、

いまもからかわれることはあるけど、

そういうときは、

「あなたにも同じ血管があるのよ」って説明するの。

When I was little, some kids teased me.
Sometimes kids still tease me.
But when they tease me about my veins, I tell them,
" you have veins, too. "

それでもからかうようなら、もう放っておくの。

それはわたしの問題じゃなくて、

彼らの問題だから。

If they still tease me, I leave them alone.
I know it's not my problem.
It's their problem.

プロジェリアじゃなければいいのに、なんて思わないわ。
わたしは、わたしという人間であることが幸せだし、
神様がわたしをこうお創りになったのには、
きっと理由があるはずだもの。

I've never thought what if I didn't have Progeria.
I'm happy to be who I am.
God made me who I am.
There must be a reason for that.

もしかしたら神様は、
"わたしはプロジェリアだけど、こう生きている"
ということを人に見せなさいって、
その機会をお与えになったのかもしれないって思うの。
この病気をとおして、
人を助けなさいということかもしれないって思うの。

Maybe God gave me a chance to show others how I live with Progeria.
Maybe God allowed me Progeria because He wants me to help others.

Chapter 2

♦

自分のこと

♦

About Me

わたしのことをかわいそうだって言う人がいるわ。
でも、その人たちはわたしじゃない。
だから、そう言うんだと思う。
だってわたし、自分のこと、
かわいそうだって、ちっとも思わないもの。

そんなふうに言う人たちは、
わたしの存在を知っているかもしれないけど、
プロジェリアで生きるということがどういうことで、
わたしがどんなふうに感じているか、
知らないでしょ？
でもね、
プロジェリアって、そんなに悪いものじゃないのよ。

There are some people who say they feel sorry for me.
But, you know what?
They are not me, so they don't know how I feel.
I don't feel sorry for myself.

These people may know me a little.
But they don't know what it's like to live with Progeria.
They don't know how I feel.
It's not as bad as they think.

わたしは、人の前で悲しい顔はしたくない。
笑顔でいると、みんながハッピーになるでしょ。

I don't like to be sad in front of others.
A smile makes everyone happy.

たとえば、車に乗っているとき、
歩道に立っている人が
わたしを不思議そうに見ても、
イヤな顔をするんじゃなくて、笑顔を見せるの。
そうすると、その瞬間に
相手も笑顔を返したりするのよ。

When I'm in the car, if people on the sidewalk look at me strange,
I always smile at them.
When I smile, people smile back at me right away.

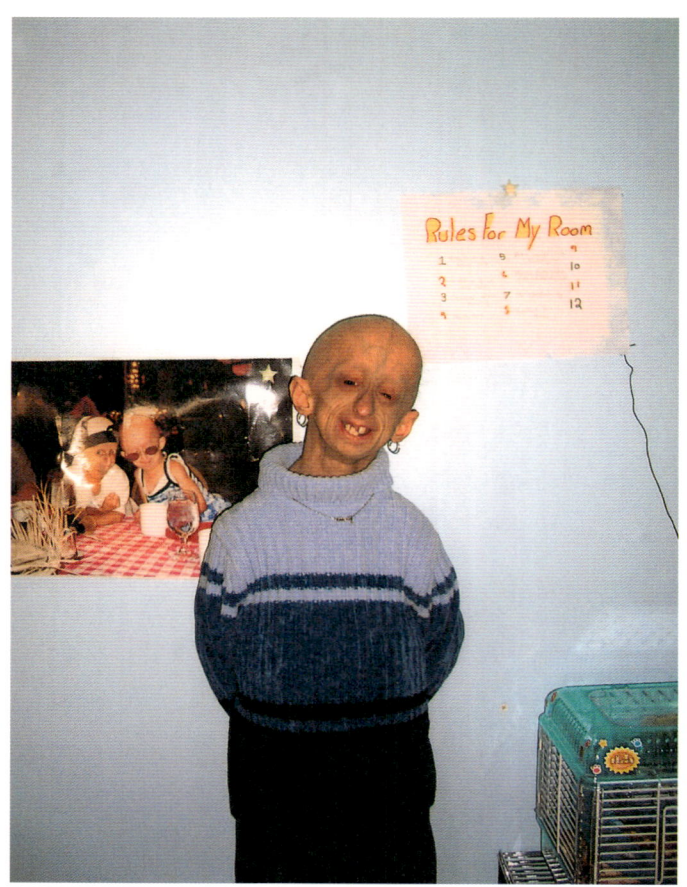

ハッピーで、面白くって、

ちょっと落ち着きがない。

自分では、自分のことをそう思ってる。

I think I'm happy, funny,
and a little bit hyper.
That's what I think I'm like.

ハッピーでいられる自分が好き。

悪口を言われたときでも、

誰かがわたしに怒ったときでも、

相手に対して怒らないでいられる自分が好き。

I like that I can always be happy.
Even if someone calls me names or gets upset with me,
I don't get mad at them.
I'm glad I can be that way.

自慢できるのは、
ハムスターの世話が上手なのと、
弟の面倒をよくみるってところ。
あと、誰かが落ち込んでいるときに、
その人をもう一度笑顔にさせるところ！

I'm good at taking care of my hamster.
I'm also good at taking care of my little brother.
And here is another thing I'm good at:
When someone is feeling down, I can make her smile again.

嫌いなところはひとつもないわ。
たまにはね、イラついちゃうときがあって、
ちょっと嫌いになりそうになるけど、
そういうときは、
なぜ、わたしは怒っているんだろうって考えて、
気持ちを落ち着けるようにしているの。
そうすると、こんなことで怒るなんて意味がない、
バカみたいだって思えてくるの。
で、それで終わりにするの。

There isn't anything that I don't like about myself.
Sometimes though, when I'm upset, I almost dislike myself.
If that happens, I try to calm down and think about what made me upset.
Then when I settle down, I can see how stupid it was to get upset.
Then I can get over it.

わたしはいつも前向きでいたい。
前向きになれないときが
これまでに一回か二回はあったかも。
でも、ほとんどないな。

I'd like to be positive all the time.
There were one or two times in my life
when I couldn't be positive.
But the rest of the time I have been.

自信を失ったこともないわよ。
だって、自信を失わされるようなことが
起こったことなんてないもの。

I haven't lost my confidence, either.
That's because nothing has ever happened
to make me lose my confidence.

人はこうなのに、自分はこうだとか、
誰かと自分を比べて、どうこう考えたりしない。
誰だって完璧じゃないもの。

I don't compare myself to others, like,
she can do this but I can't.
No one is perfect.

くじけそうになることもないな。
さみしくなることはあるけど。
さみしくなっちゃったら、音楽を聴いたり、
ママとパパと一緒にゲームをしたり、
テレビゲームをしたり、
何かをして気を紛らわせるの。
とにかく人と一緒にいるようにしているわ。

I don't really get depressed, either.
I get lonely sometimes, though.
When I feel lonely, I usually play games with my mom and dad,
listen to music, play video games, or just do stuff.
I just kinda hang out with people, you know?

悲しい映画を観たりして泣くことはあるけど、

わたしは、ふだんはあんまり泣かない。

悲しくて泣きたくなっちゃったら、

静かな場所で悲しい気持ちがおさまるのを待つの。

一人になってお祈りをしていると、

だんだん気持ちが静まってくるの。

だから泣かないですむのよ。

When I watch sad movies, I cry.
But I don't usually cry in front of people.
If I feel like crying, I go to a quiet place like my room and pray.
When I pray alone, it calms me down and I don't need to cry.

ひどいことを言われて相手に怒りを感じたときは、
その人に怒り返さないように、自分に待ったをかけるの。
そこにいたらきっと言い返してしまうから、
「ちょっと失礼」って別の場所に行って、
一拍置くようにしているの。

一拍置いて、いま起きたことを考えてみると、
憤りが相手にそう言わせたんだってことが見えてきて、
自分のなかの怒りや悲しみが消えていくの。

人が怒っているとき、相手に対して、
本心から思っているんじゃないようなことまで
勢いで言ってしまったりすることがあると思うの。
言い争いするときって、
売り言葉に買い言葉になっちゃうでしょ。
そんな怒りのシーソーゲームを続けていても、
なんにもならないじゃない？
だから、こうしようって決めたの。

When someone says something that upsets me,
I say, "excuse me," to the person,
and go somewhere to take a moment.
If I don't walk away, I will say something back to the person.

If I take a moment and think about what really happened,
I can see the reason why the person said it.
Maybe it was just because the person was angry.
Once I can see that, I don't feel upset anymore.

When people get upset, they say things that they don't mean to.
When people argue, they exchange bad words and anger.
That never gets anyone anywhere.
That's why I decided to act the way I do.

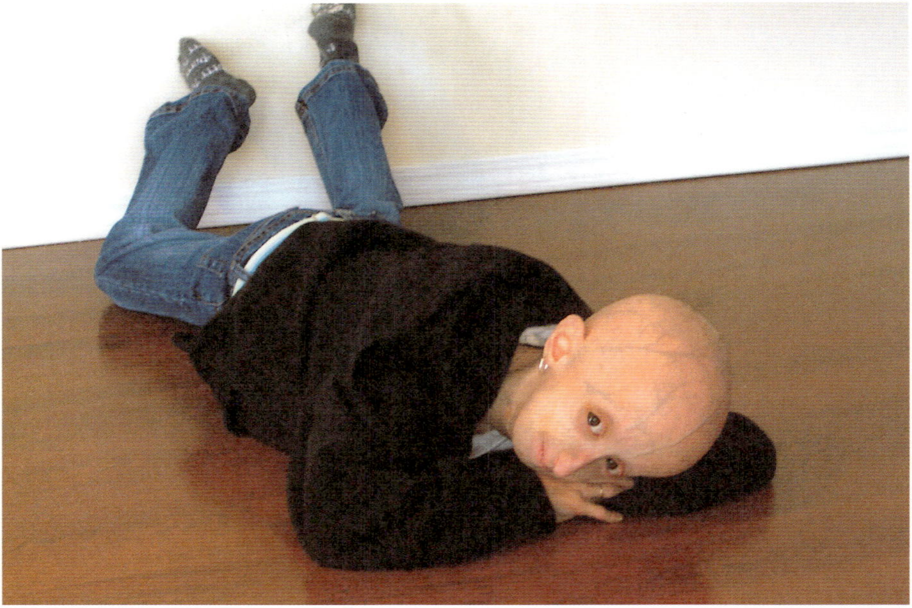

小さいころといまとでは、自分自身変わったと思う。
どんなときでもママに頼るってことがなくなったし、
自分が抱えている問題は、
自分で解決できるようになった。
つまり、もっと自立できるようになったってことよね。

I think I've grown up a lot.
I don't need my mom all the time anymore.
I'm able to solve my own problems.
That means I'm becoming independent.

Chapter 3

わたしの家族

Family

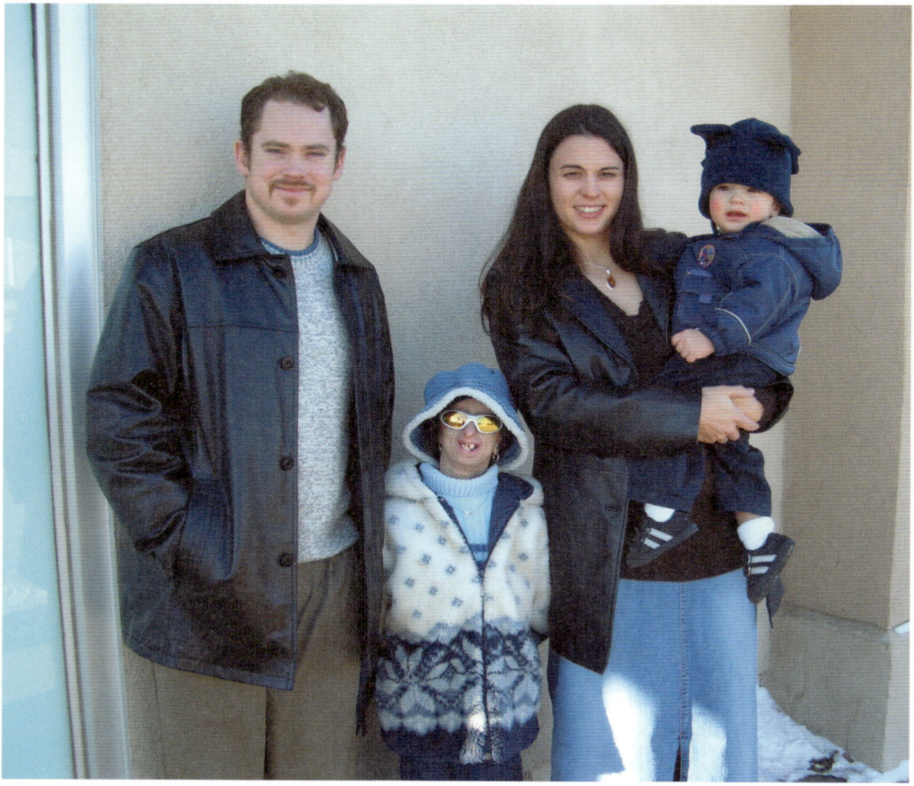

わが家は、

ママとパパ、そして弟のエヴァンの四人家族。

家族をすごく愛しているわ。

There are four of us in my family: Mom, Dad, Evan, and myself.
I love my family very much.

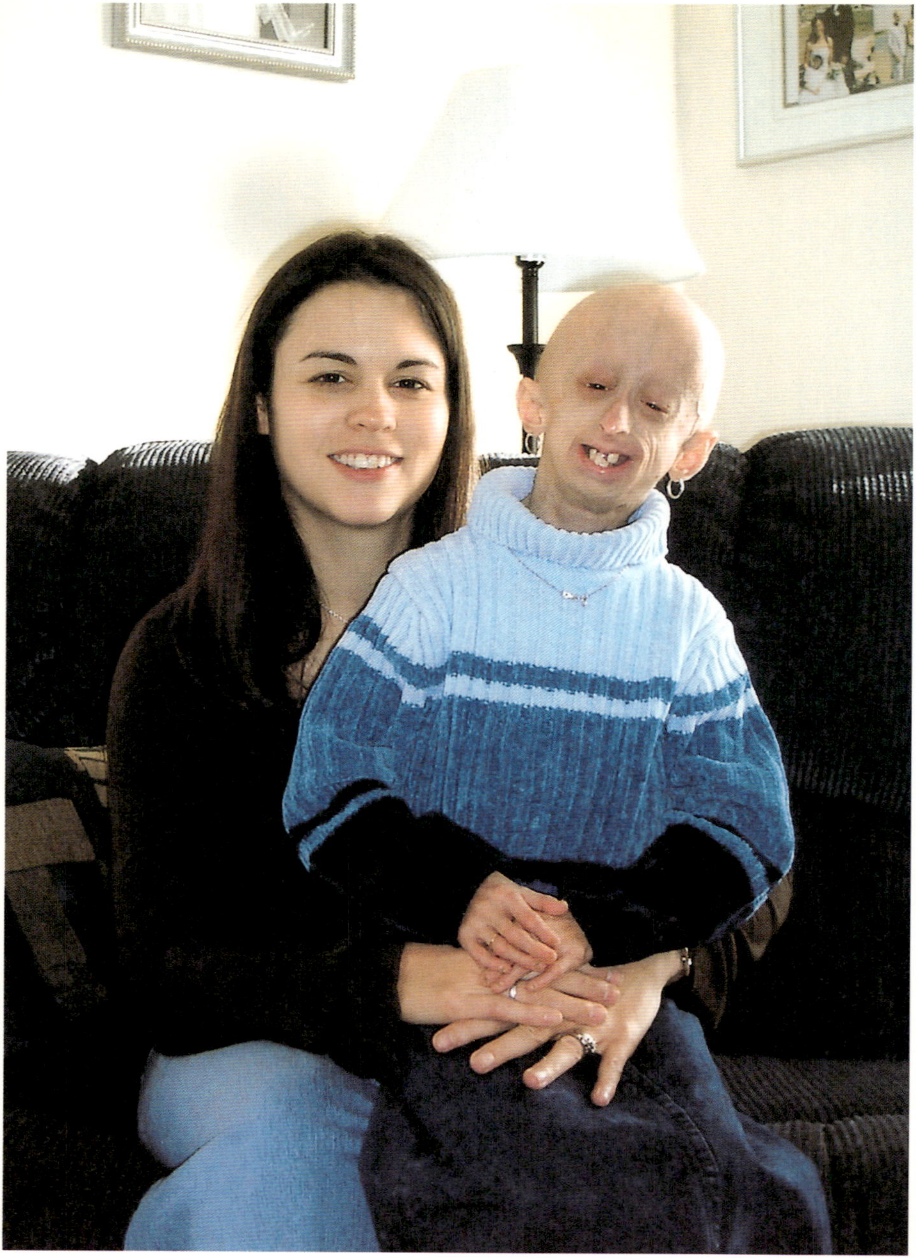

ママの名前はロリー。
ママはハッピーパーソンで、エネルギッシュで面白い人。
強い人だとも思うわ。
それに、とってもキレイなのよ。

いまは、パパと弟ができたけど、
長い間ずっと二人きりで生きてきたから、
ママはわたしの人生の一部。
わたしの人生のなかで大きな位置を占める存在なの。
ママがいなかったら、どうしていいかわからないわ。

My mom's name is Lori.
She is a happy person; energetic, funny, and strong.
And she is very pretty.

Before Mom got married, we were just the two of us.
So we've always had a very close relationship.
Mom is a big part of my life.
I don't know where I would be without her.

わたしがママより早く死んでしまうってことを、
ママは受け入れられなかったんだと思う。
以前はとても苦しそうだったわ。

そんな厳しい時期を送っていたころには、
たまに、こんなことしなきゃいいのに、
と思うようなこともあったけど、
ママはそんなときでも、わたしを愛してくれていた。
わたしもいつも、ママの助けになりたい、
何かわたしにできることはないかしら、と思っていた。

A while ago, my mom had a tough time.
She thought that I was going to die, and she was going to lose me.
It was very painful for her.

Back then, sometimes I thought like,
" I wish she wouldn't do that, " but no matter what happened,
she loved me very much.
I always wanted to help her out.
I wished there was something I could do for her.

でもいまは、ママは信仰を得て、

たとえわたしが先に死んでも、

天国で会えるんだからなんの心配もいらないってわかって、

苦しい時期を乗り越えたの。

いつの日か、天国でまた会えるんだもの。

嘆かなくていいのよ。

Since God saved Mom,
she doesn't worry about me dying anymore.
She made it through her tough times.
Now she knows that she will see me in heaven
even if I die before her.
We will see each other again one day,
so we don't need to be sad about it.

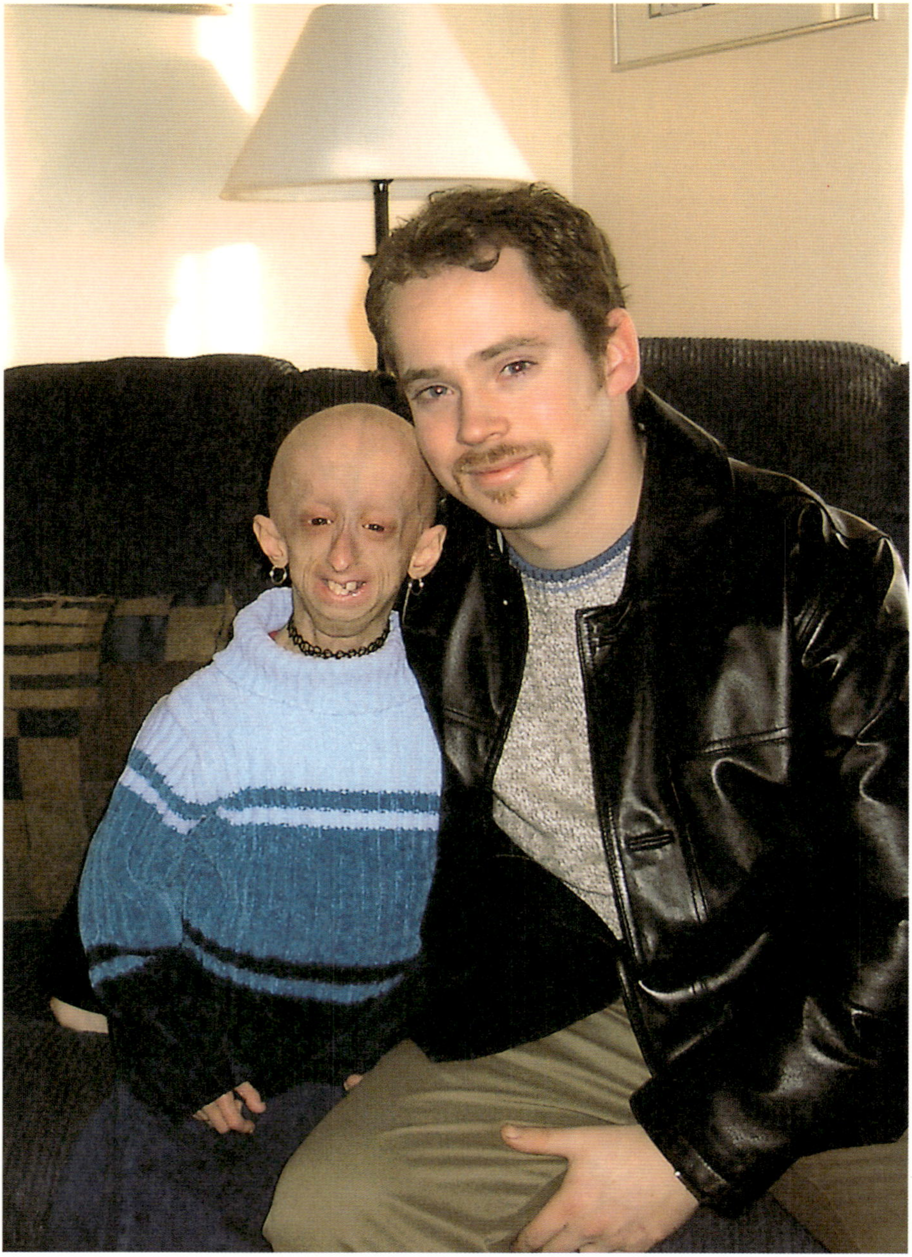

パパの名前はジェイ。
パパは面白いのよ。
冗談ばっかり言ってるわ。

パパができるって、もちろんうれしかったけど、
最初はちょっぴり不安もあったの。
でも、一緒に暮らす日々のなかで、
毎日どんどん親しくなっていって、
わたしたちは本当の家族になったの。

My dad's name is Jay.
He is funny and likes to joke around.

I was very excited to have a dad,
but a little bit anxious, too.
Having lived together for years,
we are getting closer day by day.
He is my dad and I am thankful that he is here.

二人が結婚するきっかけを作ったのは、わたしなのよ。
だって、わたしが「ジェイっていい感じだよね」って言うと、
ママったら、「私も大好き！」って口走ったの。
それで、何人かでハイキングに行ったときに、
車の窓に「ママはジェイが好き」って
イタズラ書きをしてハートマークで囲んだの。
それを一緒に車に乗っていた人に見られちゃったのよ。
それがきっかけ。

結婚式の日は、わたしも興奮しちゃった。
わたしもドレスを着て、
ママとパパのフラワーガールをやったのよ。

I was sort of a cupid for my mom and dad.
When Mom and I were talking about him,
she let the words slip out, " I like him. "
That's how I knew the way she felt about him.
When we were in the car on the way back from hiking,
I wrote on the steamed-up window, " Mommy likes Jay " with a heart.
A friend of Dad's saw it, and he told Dad about it.
That's how Dad found out about Mom's feelings toward him.

On their wedding day, I got so excited.
I was their flower girl, and I wore a white dress.

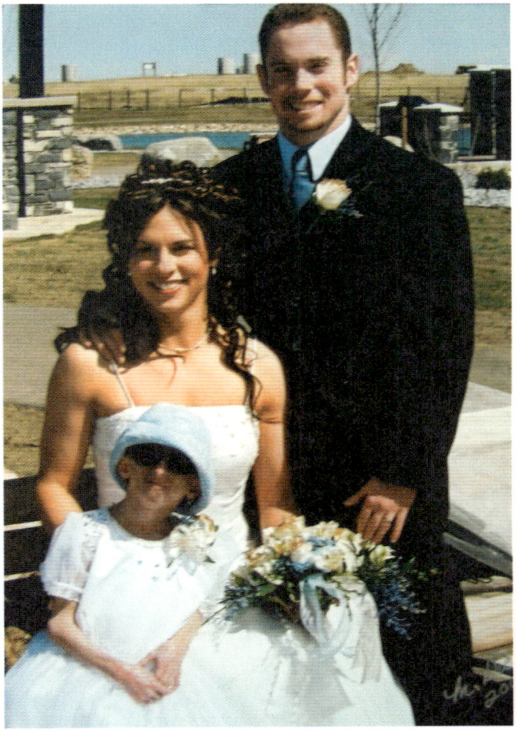

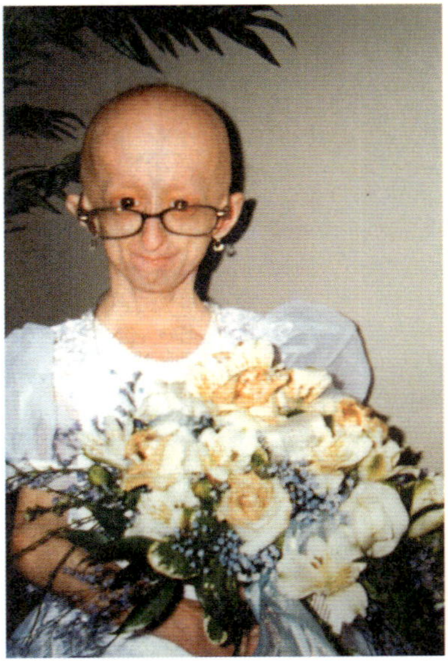

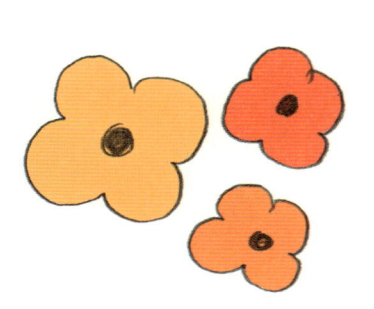

ママとパパが結婚してよかったなと思うのは、
ママが全部やらなくてもよくなって、
パパとシェアできるようになったこと。
そして、宿題でわからないところがあったら、
ママの手がはなせないときはパパに聞けるとか、
わたしにとっても、
いままでかなわなかったことができるようになったこと。

I think one of the good things about their getting married is that
Mom doesn't need to do everything by herself anymore.
She can share with Dad.
When I need help with my homework, for example, if Mom is busy, I can ask Dad.
I've got a lot of things from their marriage that I didn't have before.

家族が増えて、家での決まりごともいろいろできて、
わたしの仕事も前より増えたけど、
パパはわたしにベストだと思われることを
言ってくれるの。
厳しいときもあるけど、パパには感謝しているわ。

With a new addition to the family, there are new rules in the house,
and it's more work for me than before.
But Dad always wants the best for me and I respect that.
I am thankful for what he has done for us.

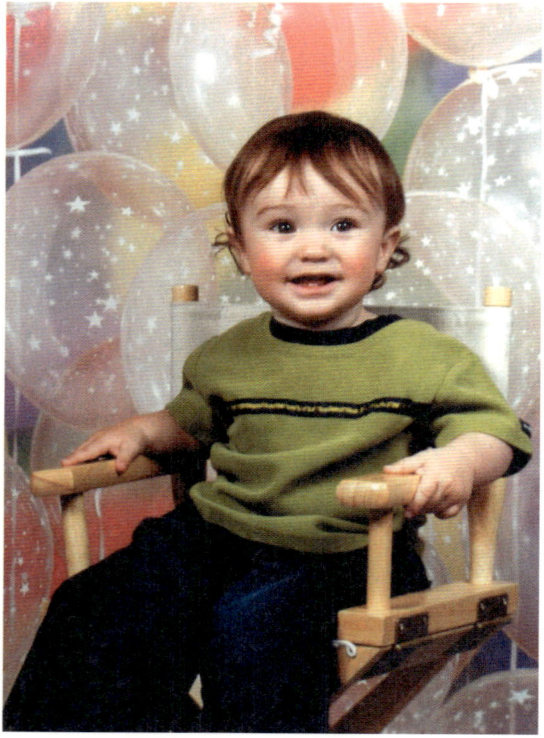

弟のエヴァンは2004年7月1日生まれで、
いま、1歳半。

ずっと弟か妹がほしかったから、
お姉ちゃんになるって聞いたときは、ワクワクしたわ。
病院ではじめて対面したとき、本当にかわいくって、
ひと目で彼のことが好きになったわ。

My brother, Evan, was born on July 1, 2004.
He is one-and-a-half years old.

When I was told that I would be a big sister,
I was really happy and excited
because I had always wanted to have a brother or sister.
When I first saw Evan at the hospital, he was so cute.
I loved him at first sight.

エヴァンはキュートでファニー。
あの子の世話をするのは、すっごく大変なの。
弟は水遊びが大好きなんだけど、
こうしないとこぼれるわよって教えてあげようとしても、
ぜったい言うことを聞かないの。
もう、ギャーってなっちゃう。
わたしが思うに、彼はわたしを困らせるのが好きなの。

Evan is very cute and funny, but he is a lot of work!
He likes to play with water.
So when I tried to teach him how to dump water in a bucket,
he wouldn't let me show him.
Then I went, "Eeeeee!!!"
I think he likes to give me a hard time.

◆057◆

弟に伝えたいのは、

わたしが彼のお姉ちゃんであることがうれしいってこと。

I'm glad to be his big sister.

とにかく弟には幸せになってほしい。

人の気持ちがわかる愛らしい子に育ってほしいと思う。

大きくなったら、何になってほしいとか、

そんなふうには考えないわ。

何でも、自分のなりたい職業についてほしい。

本当にそれで十分。

I want him always to be happy.
I want him to be a loving person, and to care about others.
There is nothing in particular that I want him to be when he grows up.
I want him to be whatever he wants to be.
Whatever he wants to be, I will be very happy.

Chapter 4

◆

わたしの一日

◆

Daily Life

朝8時に目覚まし時計をセットしてあるんだけど、
起きられなくて、いつも8時半までベッドにいるの。
それからシャワーを浴びて、身支度をして朝食。
時間があるときはメールをチェックしたりして、
9時半には家を出るの。
学校はすぐ近くだから、
着いてすぐ9時50分からの授業に出席するの。
授業は、1時限目はパスして2時限目から受けているの。
だけど、最近は体調がよくって、
そのあとは最後まで授業に出ているのよ。

My alarm clock is set for 8 a.m. but I usually stay in bed until about 8:30.
Then I take a shower, get dressed, and eat breakfast.
When I have time after breakfast, I check my e-mail.
I leave the house for school around 9:30.
The school is close to my house
so I can catch second period, which starts at 9:50.
I usually skip first period, but since I've been feeling great lately,
I've been attending all the rest of my classes.

学校が午後3時10分に終わるから、

帰宅するのは、3時20分から30分くらいね。

家に帰ってきてからは、日によって違うけど、

コンピュータに向かったり、テレビを見たり、

弟と遊んだり、バイブルを読んだり、

宿題があれば宿題をするわ。

もちろん、ママのお手伝いもするわよ。

そのあとは、家族で夕食を食べて、

夜は両親とボードゲームをやったりして、

平日は、10時にベッドに入る。

わたしの一日は、だいたいこんな感じかしら。

The school day ends at 3:10 p.m.,
so I get home between 3:20 and 3:30.
What I do after school depends on the day.
I usually play on the computer, watch TV, play with my brother, read my bible,
or do homework if I have any.
Of course I help my mom, too.
Then, I eat supper with my family.
Sometimes after supper, I play board games with my parents.
I go to bed around 10 on school nights.
That's pretty much what a normal day is like.

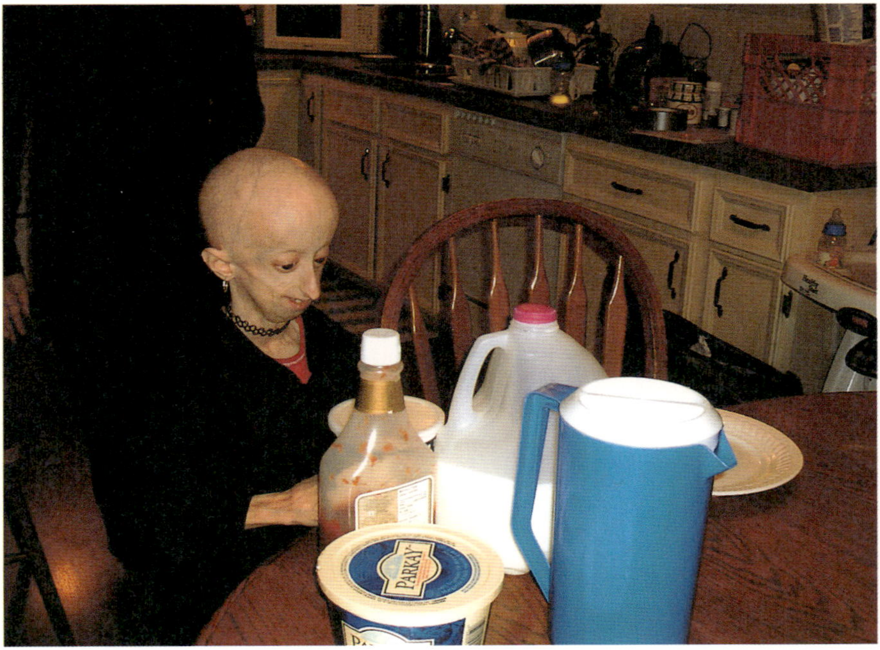
PARKAY

曜日ごとに決まった予定も入っているのよ。
火曜日は近所のチャーチグループの集まり、
水曜日は教会でチャーチミーティングがあるの。
そして、木曜日はおじいちゃんちに遊びに行く日。
でも、ウイークデイだから泊まれないの。
おばあちゃんちに遊びに行く金曜日は、
週末だからお泊まりをするの。
わたしはアイスホッケーの
シーズンチケットをもっているので、
ホームゲームがあるときは二人で見に行くのよ。
おばあちゃんとわたしは趣味が合うの。
だからわたし、金曜日が大好きなの。

I have a pretty regular schedule each week.
On Tuesday evenings, I have bible study.
Then on Wednesday evenings,
I have a prayer meeting.
I visit Poppy on Thursday nights
but can't stay over since it's a school night.
On Friday nights,
I visit Nanny and stay over there since it's the weekend.
And whenever our hockey team plays at home,
we always go to see the game
because I have season tickets.
Nanny likes the things I like;
we have kind of the same taste.
Fridays are a lot of fun.

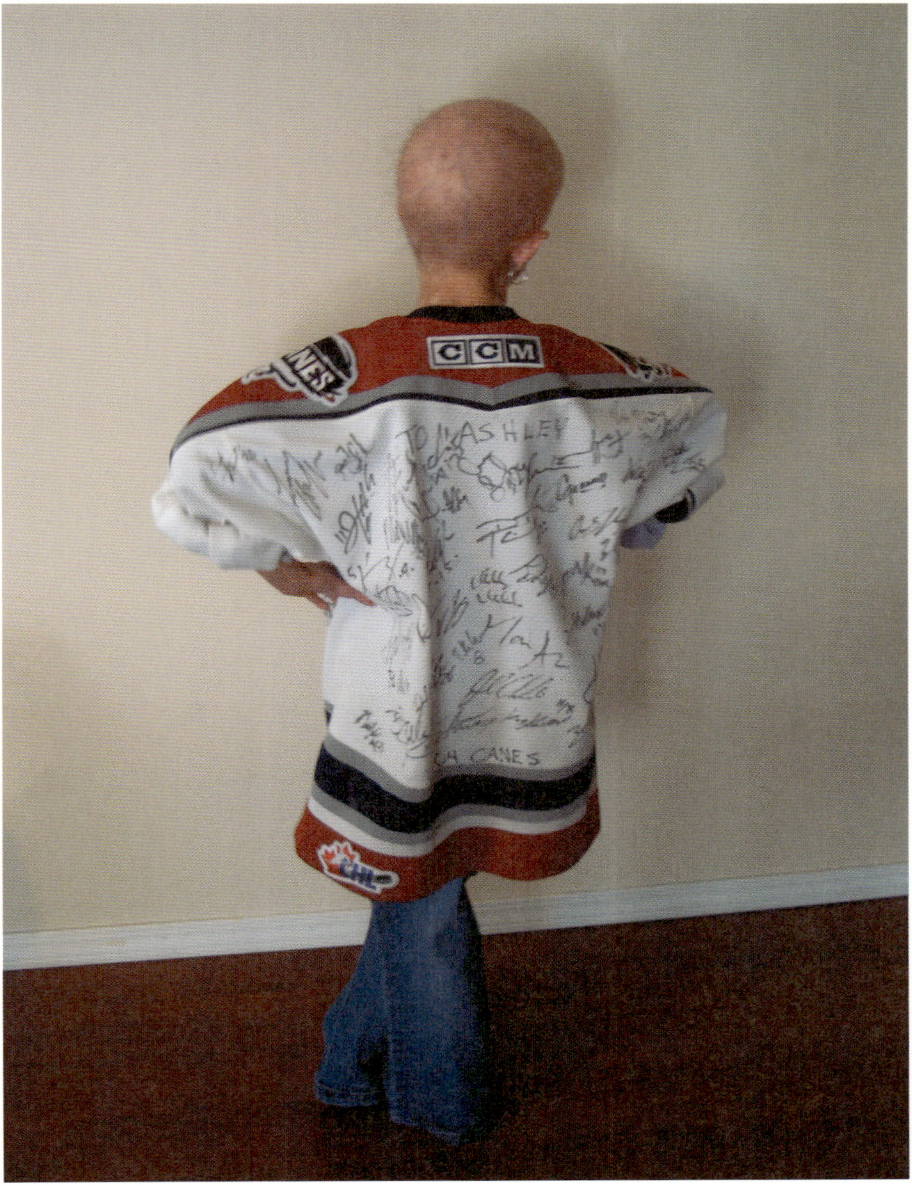
CCM
TO ASHLEY
CHL

週末は、ハムスターと遊ぶのが好き。

絵を描いたりすることもあるし、

弟ともたくさん遊んであげる。

家族で食事に行くこともあるのよ。

ミニゴルフとか映画に出かけることもあるわね。

ネイルサロンに行ったりもするのよ。

行くのは1カ月おきくらいかな。

わたし、青と紫が好きなの。

だから青のネイルをするんだ。

I do different things on the weekends.
I like to play with my hamster, and draw pictures.
I can play with my little brother
longer than I can during the week.
Sometimes I eat out, play mini golf,
or go to the movie theater with my family.

I go to the nail salon every other month.
I like to get my nails done in blue.
My favorite colors are blue and purple.

大きな胸の痛みは、ここ一年くらい起こっていないの。
だけど、頭痛はそれなりにひんぱんにあって、
そういうときは起きるのがツライ。
でも、頭痛がある日もがんばって学校には行くのよ。
だけど、お昼までに治まらなかったら早退して、
家に帰って寝ることにしているの。
ときには点滴を受けなきゃ治らないときもあるけど、
たいてい、午後4時くらいまで寝て起きると、
だいぶよくなっているのよ。
それでも治らなかったら、また寝るの。

頭痛があっても、薬を飲んで寝るしか方法がないの。
だから、痛みのことは考えないようにするの。
そうすると、いつのまにか頭痛はどこかに消えてしまう。

こんな感じで、頭痛があっても普通に暮らしているのよ。
みんなと違うのは、ちょっとお昼寝をするってことくらいね。

I haven't had chest pains in maybe a year.
Headaches, I get every now and then.
When I have a headache,
it's tough to wake up but I usually go to school anyway.
If it doesn't get better by noon, I go back home and take a nap.
Usually if I take a nap until about four o'clock, it gets better.
If it doesn't, I just sleep more.
Sometimes, though, I have to get an IV.

All I can do when I get a headache is to take some medicine and a nap,
so I try not to think about it.
If I don't think that I have a headache, it will go away.

I just live like I usually would.
The only difference is that I have to take a nap.

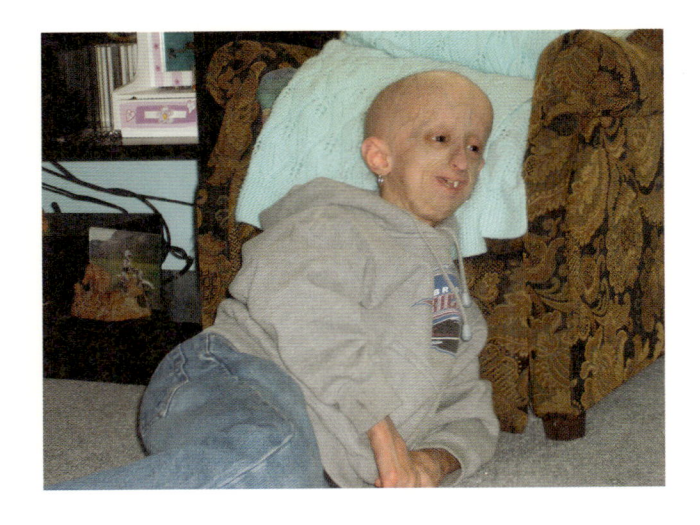

Chapter 5

♦

お気に入り

♦

Favorite Things

好きな言葉は

「PEACE」「LOVE」「JOY」「SWEET」「SMILE」!

ステキな言葉よね。

あと、「SASSY」っていうのも好き。

「生意気」とかいう意味なんだけど、私は好きなの。

友だちはみんな私のこと、「SASSY」だって言うのよ。

アハハ、けっこうあたってるかも。

My favorite words are Peace, Love, Joy, Sweet, and Smile.
Those are good words.
I also like the word, Sassy,
which means lively, spirited, and impish.
My friends sometimes call me Sassy and I guess it's kinda right!

PEACE

LOVE

JOY

Sweet

Smile

ママの作るスパゲティが好き。

おばあちゃんのラザニアが好き。

コーラが好き。

チョコレートバーが好き。

果物では、イチゴとスイカと……バナナも好き。

とくに、スイカが大好物なの。

いっつもおなか痛くなっちゃうくらい食べちゃうんだ。

食いしん坊だって思わないでね。

みんなだって、そうでしょ？

I like the spaghetti that my Mom makes.
I like the lasagna that Nanny makes.
I like Pepsi.
I like crunchy chocolate bars.
I like strawberries, watermelons, and bananas.
In the hot days of summer, I eat a lot of watermelon,
till my stomach starts hurting.
I am pretty sure you like these things, too.

わが家のペットを紹介するわ。
いま飼っているのは、
ロットワイラー・ジャーマンシェパードのサムソンと
ジャーマンシェパードのセイバー。
セイバーは最近ウチの一員になったばかりの子犬よ。

ハムスターのナゲットも忘れちゃいけないわね。

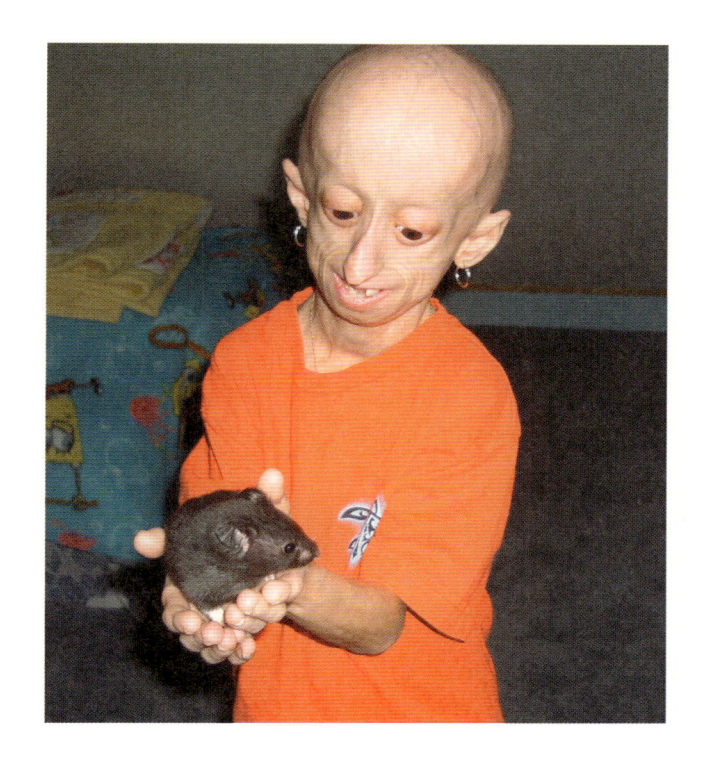

I would like to introduce my pets.
I have a Rottweiler-German shepherd mix whose name is
Samson and a German shepherd whose name is Saber.
Saber is a puppy and has recently joined my family.

Nugget is my hamster.
Don't forget about him although he is small.

動物が大好き！

ペットショップで働けたらいいなあ。

そうしたら、ずっと動物と一緒にいられるでしょ。

毎日きっと楽しいだろうなあと思う。

I love animals!
I wonder if I can work at a pet store.
If I can, I can be with lots of animals every day.
It would be so fun to work there.

動物の世話だって、ちゃんと自分でするわよ。

でも、イヌはどんどん大きくなっちゃうでしょ？

お散歩とかが大変。

わたしの力では世話できなくなっちゃうんだ。

ハムスターだったら、ずっと自分で世話ができるけどね。

I like taking care of animals.
But dogs grow bigger quickly so it is pretty tough to take them for walks by myself.
Once they become big, they are stronger than me.
I can take care of hamsters, though.

ネコも大好きよ。
わたしのタイプの動物って感じ。

I love cats, too.
They are my kind of animal.

趣味もいっぱいあるわよ。
キャンプやミニ四駆とかね。
ミニ四駆はヘルメットをかぶって乗る四輪車なんだけど、
おじいちゃんと一緒にやるの。
コンピューターや映画も趣味だな。
好きな映画スターとかは別にいないけど、
最近観たなかでは、『僕はラジオ』って映画がよかったわよ。

I have a lot of hobbies.
Riding on my Quad. Going camping...
When I ride on the Quad, which has four wheels,
I have to wear a helmet like a racing driver.
Usually, my grandpa takes me to ride the Quad.
I like playing with the computer and watching movies, too.
Although I don't have any favorite movie stars,
the movie called <u>RADIO</u> that I watched recently was pretty good.

趣味とはいえないけど、長電話もよくする。
「元気にしてる？　最近どう？」なんて感じで、
とりとめもないおしゃべりをするのが好き。
相手の時間が許せば、1時間くらいはおしゃべりしちゃうな。

I don't know if it is my hobby but I like to talk on the phone.
" Hi! How are you? What's new? "
I just like rambling with my friends and relatives on the phone.
If they have time to talk, I can even go on for an hour!

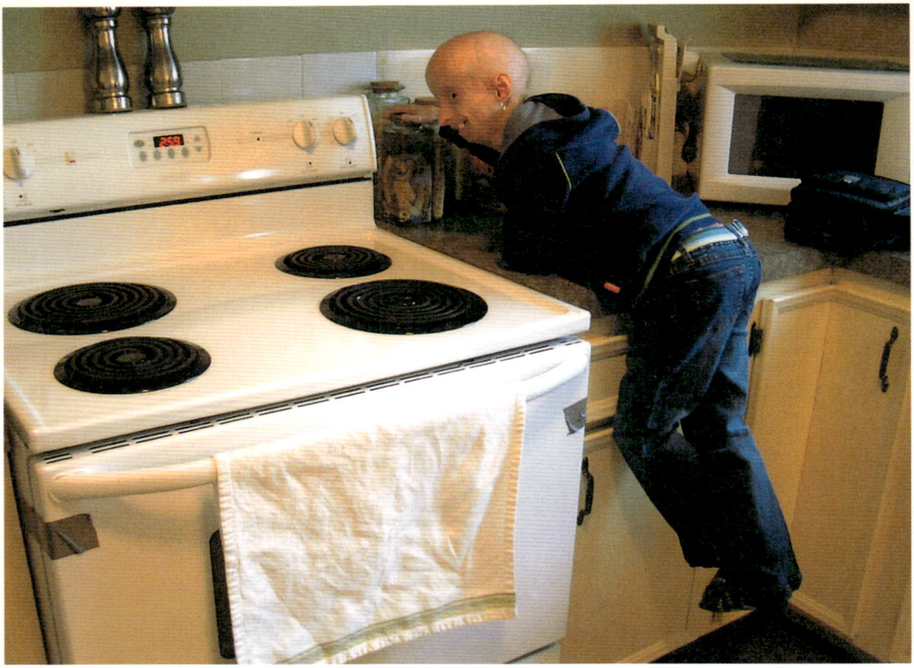

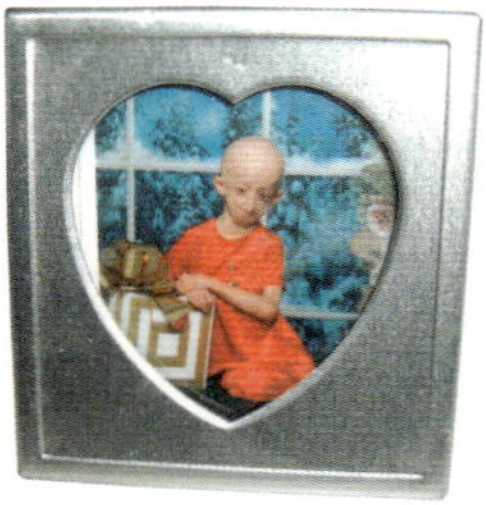

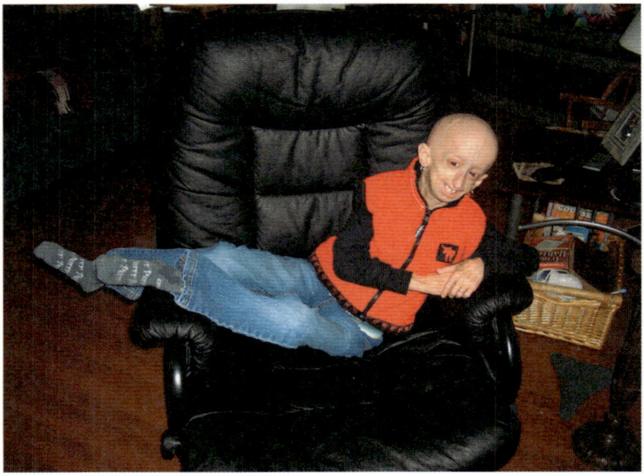

お転婆なこともけっこう好きなの。
でもね、女のコらしいところもあるから、
どっちの面もあるって感じだと思う。
両方のちょうど真ん中くらいってとこじゃないかな。

だから、お洋服も、Tシャツとジーンズのときもあるし、
ドレスアップしてちゃんとスカートをはくときもある。

I am kind of a tomboy but I also like girly stuff, too.
I think I am between a tomboy and girly.
Maybe I am just in the middle.

Because of it, sometimes I wear a pair of blue jeans and a T-shirt.
Sometimes I wear a skirt and feel dressed up.

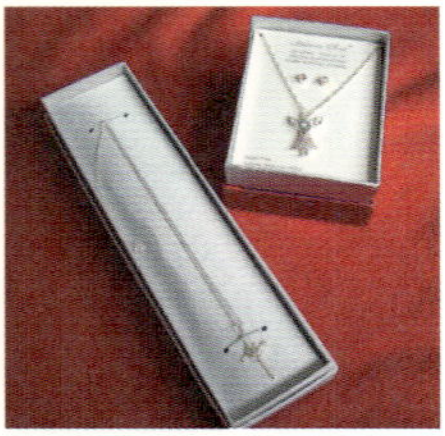

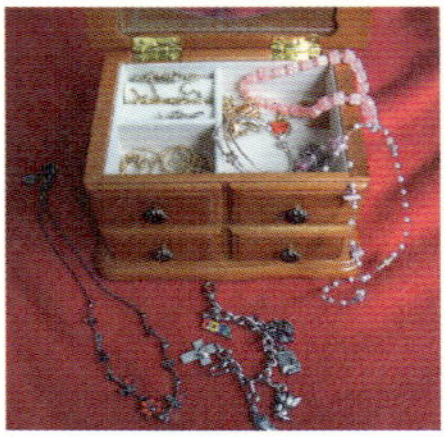

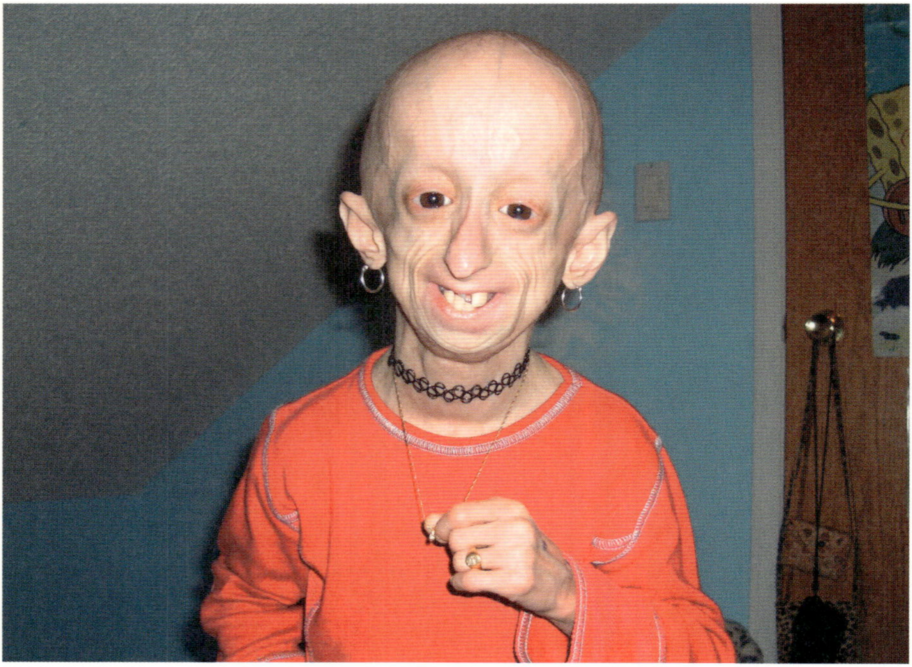

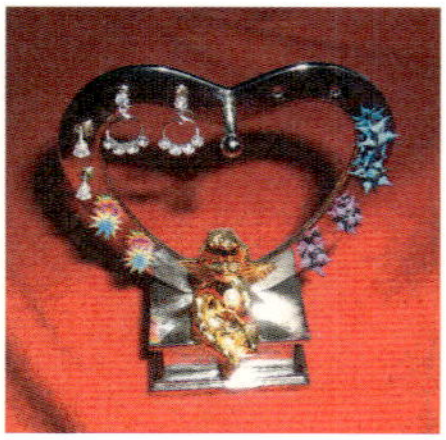

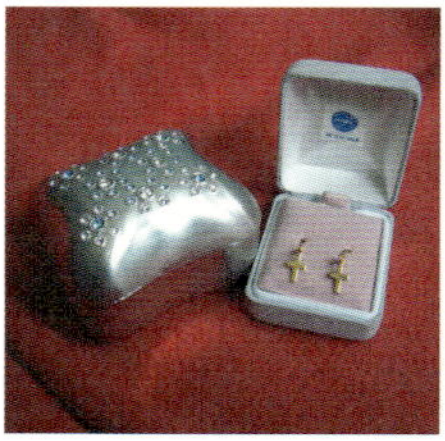

アクセサリーのオシャレが好き。
数えきれないくらいもっているんだけど、
どうしても新しいお気に入りばっかり
するようになっちゃうのよね。
いまのお気に入りは、このネックレスと指輪なの。

I like wearing accessories and jewelry.
Although there are countless things in my jewelry boxes,
I wear only my favorites or new ones anyway.
My current favorites are this necklace and these rings.

春は、暑すぎもせず、寒すぎもせず。
だんだん木々が芽吹いてくるところが好き。

夏は、暑すぎるときもあるけど、
プールに飛び込みたくなるような暑さが好き。

秋は、葉っぱの色が彩りを増すのが好き。
落ち葉の上でジャンプしたりするの。

冬は、雪が木とかに積もったりするのが好き。
日の光にキラキラ輝いて、とってもキレイだもの。
でも、ものすごく寒いとこだけは好きになれない。

どの季節もみんなそれぞれによさがある。
だけど、ひとつ選ぶなら、そうね、やっぱり春が好き。

Spring is not hot but not cold.
I like that trees start having buds and flowers start blooming.

    Although sometimes it gets too hot in summer,
    I like it because it makes me want to jump into the swimming pool.

I like fall because it is very colorful with the turning leaves.
And I can hop on the piles of leaves.

    Looking at the snowflakes on the trees is very beautiful.
    The snow is brilliant with reflected sunshine.
    However, it is very cold here during winter.
    That is the only bad part of it.

Every season has a good part.
If I had to choose one, I would choose spring.

Chapter 6

♦

学校

♦

School

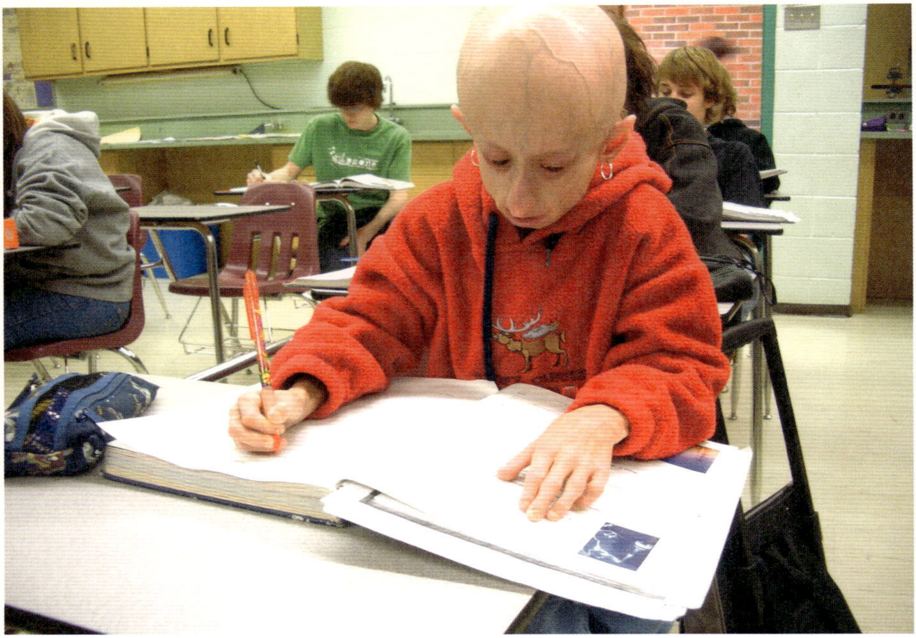

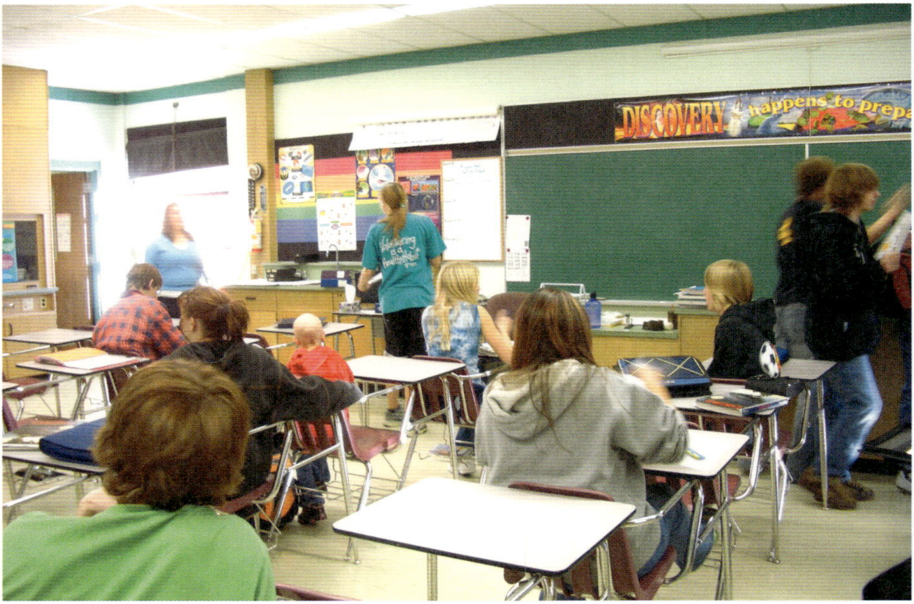
DISCOVERY happens to prepa

いまの学校のことがとっても気に入っているの。
前の学校では、
わたしだけ別のクラスで勉強させられたり、
アシスタントの先生がなんでもやってくれたり、
正直言って、ほとんど何も学ばなかった。
でも、いまの学校では、仲間と一緒に勉強できる。
そして、実際に何かを学んでいるの。
それをわたし、すごく楽しんでいるの。

今学期は、化学と数学、美術、体育をとっているの。
大好きな科目は美術。
この間も、アートの課題をいちばん早く仕上げて
誰よりも先に提出したのよ。

I really like my school.
Before I went there, I was in different classes from my friends,
and the assistant teacher did everything for me.
Honestly, I didn't learn anything.
In my new school, I can study with my friends
and am actually learning a lot of stuff.
I'm really enjoying that.

This quarter, I'm taking science, math, art, and gym.
My favorite class is art.
I was the first one in the class to turn in my assignment the other day.

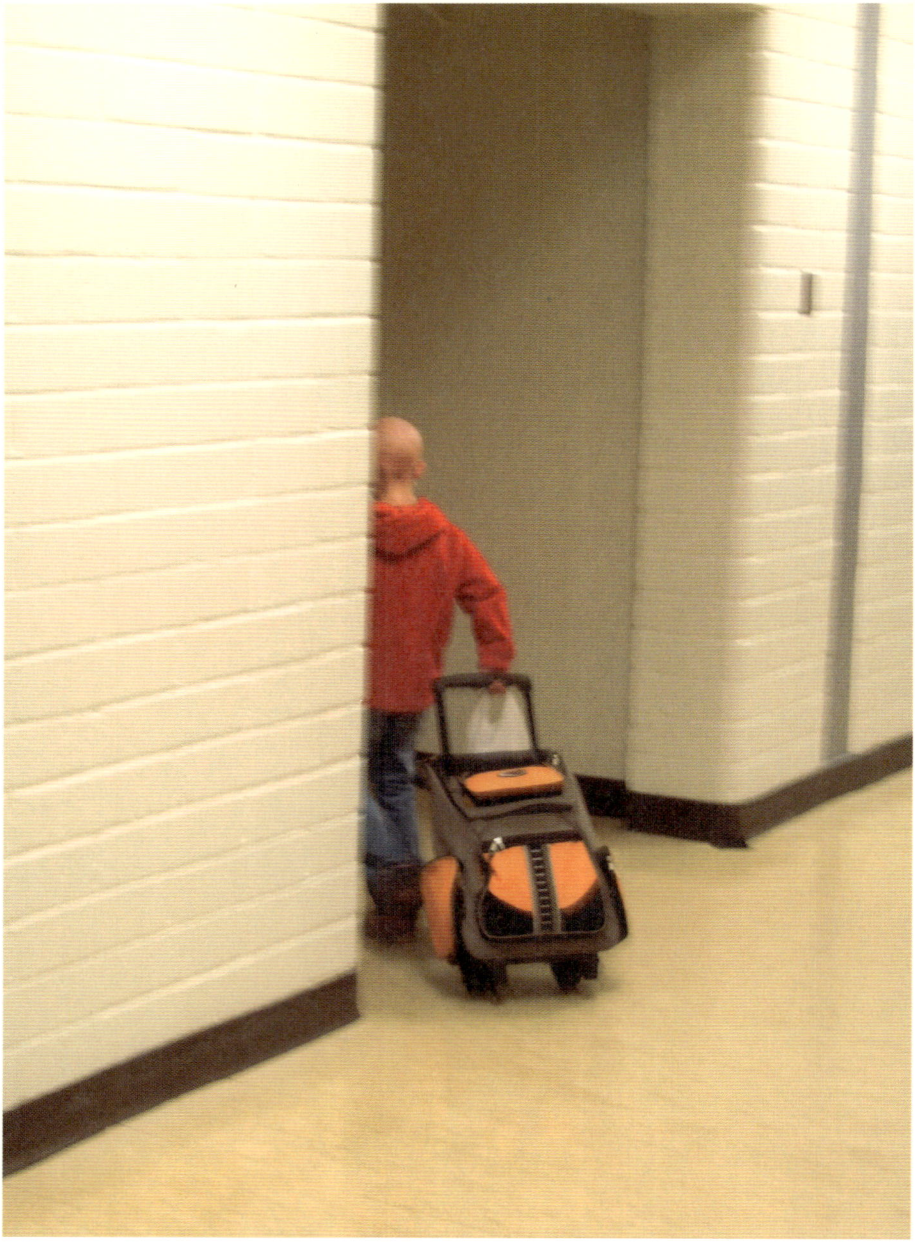

いまの学校では、
アシスタントの先生はついていないのよ。
だから、いろんなことが自分でできるようになった。
それによって自分自身が自立できたと思う。

クラスメイトの人数も多いし、
仲間からのヘルプだって得られるんだもの。
アシスタントの先生がいなくたって不安は感じないわ。
それどころか、このほうが断然好き。

教科書やテキストのバインダー、筆記用具は重いけど、
キャリーバッグに入れて、自分で持ち歩いているのよ。

In this school, I don't have an assistant teacher who takes care of me.
Because of that, I can do more on my own.
So I'm more independent than before.

Since, at this school, all the kids in my grade are in one class,
I can get more help from my classmates than before.
Although I don't have an assistant teacher, I don't feel insecure at all.
I rather like it.

Textbooks, a binder, pens, and pencils are pretty heavy.
I have a wheeled backpack so I can carry everything by myself.

学校で仲がいいのは、
ブリタニーでしょ、アッシュでしょ。
それからスティーヴンにアーロンにティナ。
ブリタニーが声をかけてくれて、
いろんなことを一緒にやるようになって、
しばらくたってから、
アーロンたちのグループに誘われたの。

お弁当を一緒に食べたり、
廊下で座り込んでおしゃべりしたり、
いつもみんなでふざけてばかりいるのよ。
たいていは、次の授業のどこがキライとかいう話で
盛り上がっているの。

At school, I hang out with Brittany, Ash, Steven, Aaron, and Tina.
Brittany told me if I ever needed help, she would help me.
So we started working in the same group.
After a little while,
Aaron asked us if we wanted to be in his group.

We eat lunch together,
and sit in the hallway talking or joking around.
What do we talk about?
We usually talk about what we don't like about the next class.

◆098◆

All photos at the school

友だちっていうのは、お話をする相手。

助けが必要なときにそばにいてくれる相手。

つまり、笑顔にさせてくれる人ってことだと思う。

**A friend is someone who talks with you
and would be there for you if you needed help.
I think if somebody makes you smile, she is your friend.**

親友っていうのは……むずかしいわね。
うーん、よくわからないけど、
ほかの誰よりも一緒に過ごす時間が
長い相手のことかなあ。
ちょっと違うかなあ。
そうだ！
長い時間をかけてお互いのことを理解しあっている人。
きっと、そんな相手のことじゃないかしら。

What is a best friend? It's hard to say...
I don't know how I should describe that,
but maybe you spend more time with the person than anyone else.
Oh! Maybe it would be a person you've known a long time,
and you have understood each other very well since you met.
Maybe that's a best friend.

Chapter 7

♦

親友

♦

Best Friend

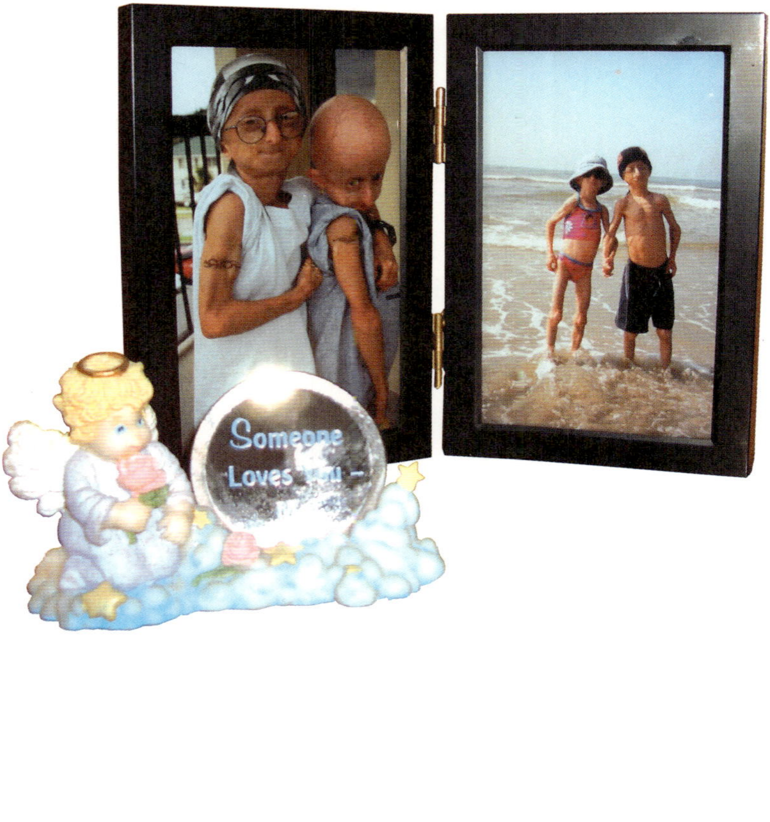
Someone
Loves You

ジョンは親友だった。
とても大切な存在だった。

わたしたちは同じ病気をもっているし、
お互いの人生に何が起こっているのか、
何も言わなくてもわかりあえていたの。

John was my best friend.
He meant a lot to me.

As we both had the same disease,
we kinda knew what was going on in each other's life.
We didn't need to talk to understand each other.

ジョンと一緒にいるときは、いつも楽しかった。

幸せな気持ちになった。

そして、そんなすばらしい友情で

結ばれているってことが、わたしはすごくうれしかった。

It was always fun to be around him.
He made me feel happy.
We had such a wonderful friendship.

彼は、わたしがへこんでいないか、
いつも気づかってくれていたの。
彼はわたしを笑わせようとしてくれたから、
彼の前でへこんだことはあまりないけど、
わたしがちょっとへこんでいるようなときは、
何も言わずにハグしてくれた。

He always made sure to know how I was feeling.
He would always try to make me laugh so I always felt fine around him.
But, if I felt a little bit down, he would just give me a hug.

楽しかった思い出がたくさんあるのよ。
一緒に過ごしたフロリダでのことなんだけど、
ジョンがウォーターバルーンをいっぱい買って、
わたしも同じようにいっぱい買って、
それをぶつけあって遊んだの。
楽しかったなあ。

I have a lot of fun memories of him.
When we went to Florida together,
John and I bought a whole bunch of water balloons at the store.
And we had a big water balloon fight.
It was so much fun!

二人とも体の大きさも似ていたから、
わたしがジョン、ジョンがわたしのフリをする
入れかわりごっこもよくしたわ。
あるときなんか、同じようにジーンズをはき、
二人とも同じＴシャツを着て、
ジョンはいつもしている眼鏡をはずして、
二人がかわりばんこに、ジョンのおばあちゃまの前を
あいさつしながら何度も走り抜けたの。
で、最後に一緒に出て行ってあいさつをしたのね。
そしたら、おばあちゃまが腰を抜かすほど驚いてね。
あれは、ホントにおかしかった。

Sometimes John pretended to be me and I pretended to be him.
One day, we both wore the same blue jeans and the same T-shirts.
We were the same size.
John always wore glasses but he took them off.
We took turns running in front of his grandma,
each time saying, "Hi, grandma! How are you?"
When we came to her together and said,
"Hi, grandma, how are you?" she almost fell out her chair.
It was the funniest moment. It still makes me laugh.

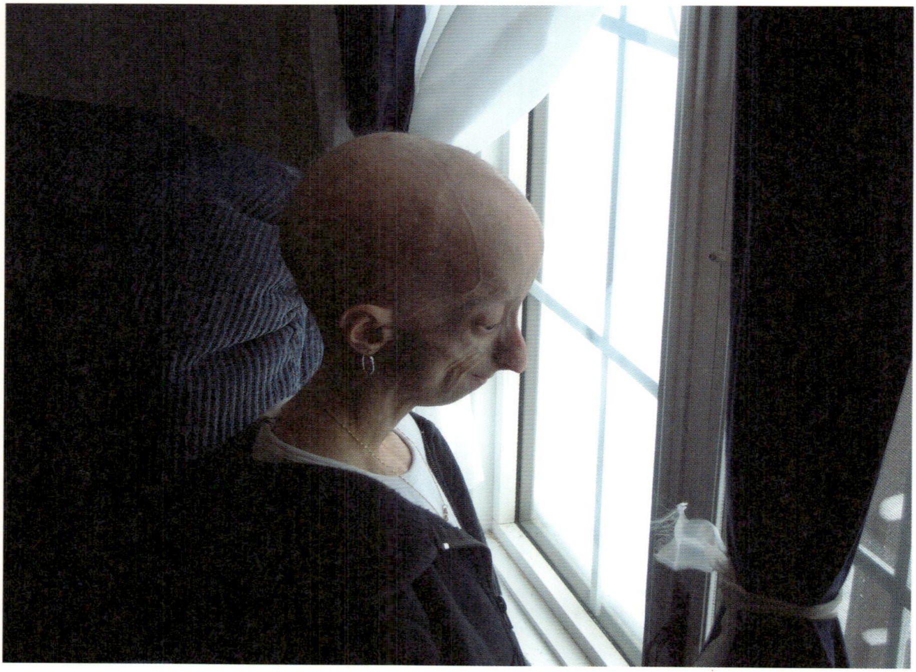

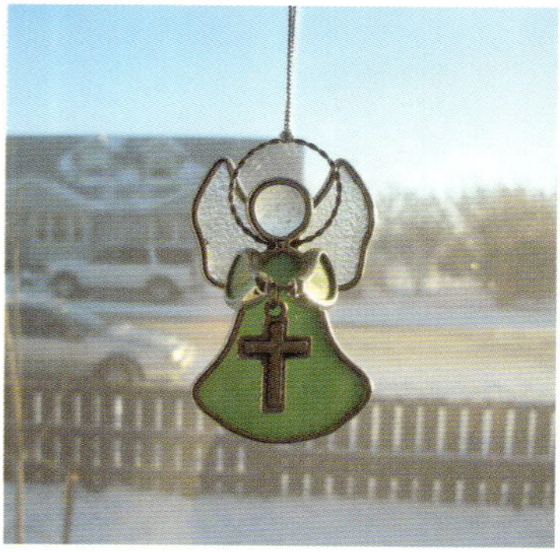

彼はいろんなことを教えてくれた。
言葉であれこれ言うんじゃなくて、
悲しんで生きるより幸せに生きようとする姿を
見せてくれたの。
大変なことが多いけど、
どう幸せに生きるかが大事なんだ、
ということを教えてくれたの。

彼からは、本当にたくさんのことを教わったわ。

John taught me a lot of things.
He taught me how to live positively by showing me, instead of telling me.
He taught me to be happy in life even when things are hard.

I learned many things from him.

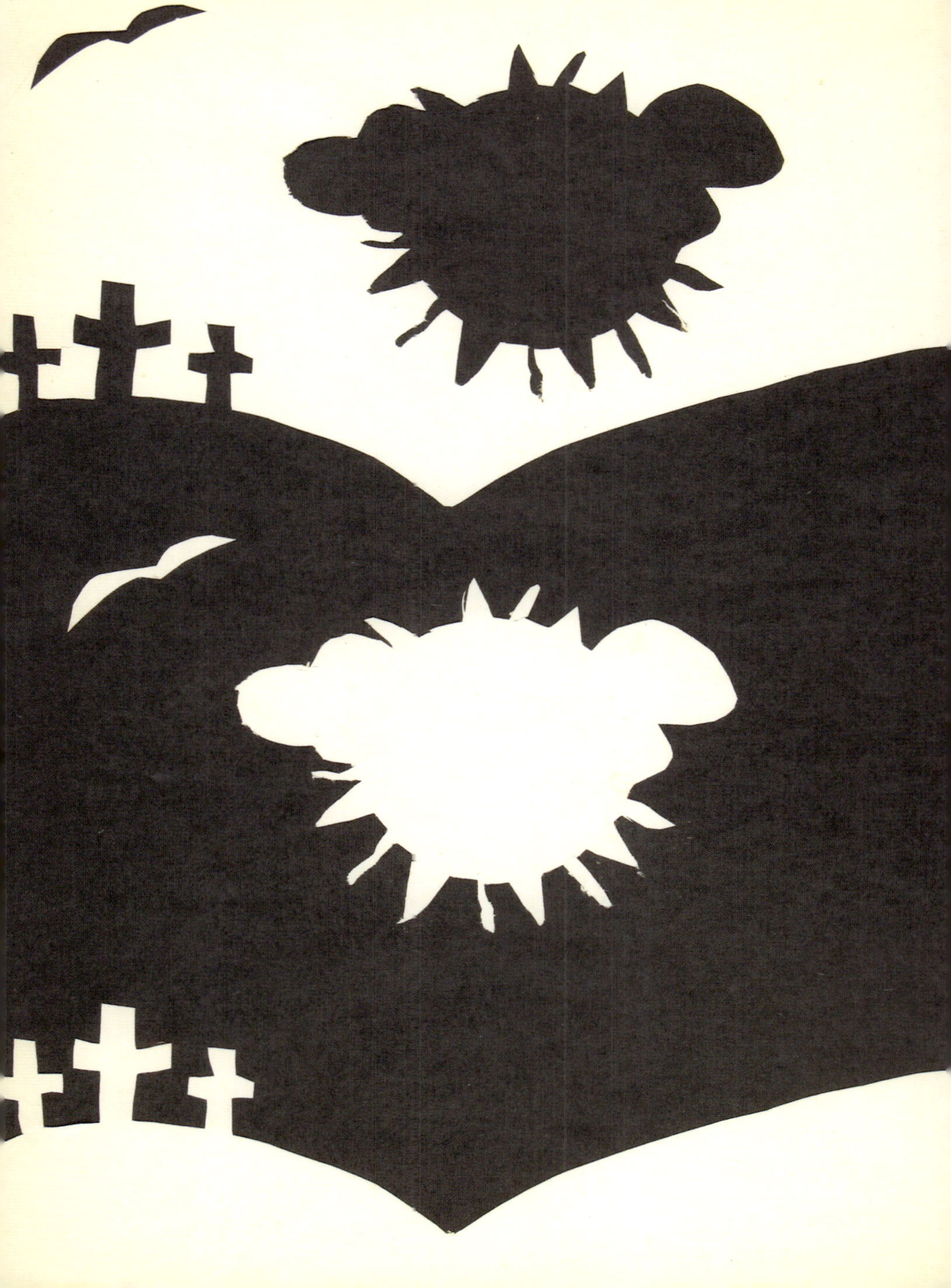

ジョンが亡くなったときは、ものすごく悲しかった。

でも、ジョンは天国というすばらしい場所に
行ったんだから悲しんじゃいけない、
わたしたちはすぐにまた会えるんだって思ったの。

When I heard that he had passed away, I was really sad.

Then I thought that I shouldn't be sad.
Because he is in a better place called Heaven
and I will see him there again someday.

彼はアメリカ、わたしはカナダに住んでいて、
めったに会えなかったけど、
いつも彼と一緒にいるって感じがしていたの。
たとえ離れていても、
彼がいつもそばにいると感じてた。
それは、いまも同じよ。

He lived in the U.S.
I live in Canada.
We couldn't see each other so often.
But I felt that I was always with him,
whether we were together or apart.
I still feel like that.

もしもいま、彼とお話ができるとしたら、
「ハーイ、どうしてる？」って言って
天国の様子を聞くわ。そして、
「あなたとそこでまた会えたらすごくステキね」
って言うわ。

If I could talk to him on the phone, I would say,
"Hi! How are you doing?" and ask him what it's like up there.
And I would tell him it would be neat to visit him again.

Chapter 8

◆

命

◆

Life

わたしは、死ぬのは怖いとは思わない。

I'm not afraid of dying.

もしも、わたしが誰かから

あなたにはあと24時間の命しかありませんよ、

と言われたとしても、

それで困ったりはしないわ。

死は誰にでも訪れるもの。

恐れるなんて、

意味がないことだと思う。

If someone told me I had only 24 hours to live,
I wouldn't be afraid.

Everyone has her own time.
I know I don't need to be afraid of dying.

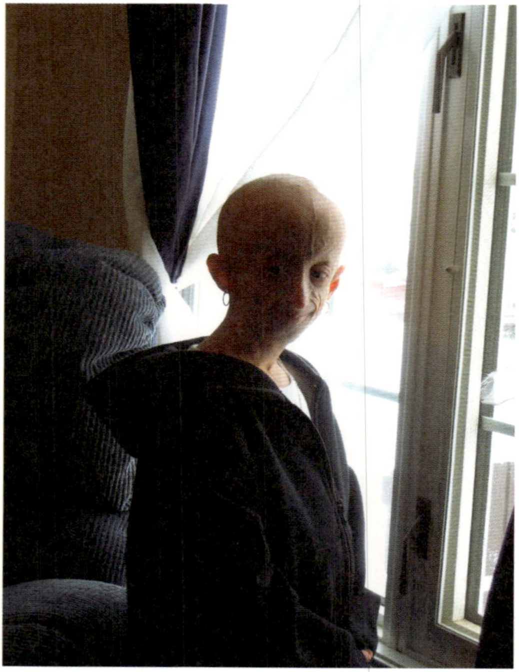

なぜ、ここにいるのか、
それはわからない。
でも、わたしたちがここにいるのには、
何か目的があるはずだと思うの。

I don't know why we are here.
But I think we are here for a reason.

わたしはハッピーに生きたい。

ほかの人たちを勇気づけるように生きたい。

I'd like to live happily.
I'd like to encourage others.

生きるチャンスを与えられているのだもの。

わたしは、自分の定められた時間がくるまで、

すこやかに生きていきたいと思っているわ。

God gives us a chance to live.
I'd like to live a healthy life until my time comes.

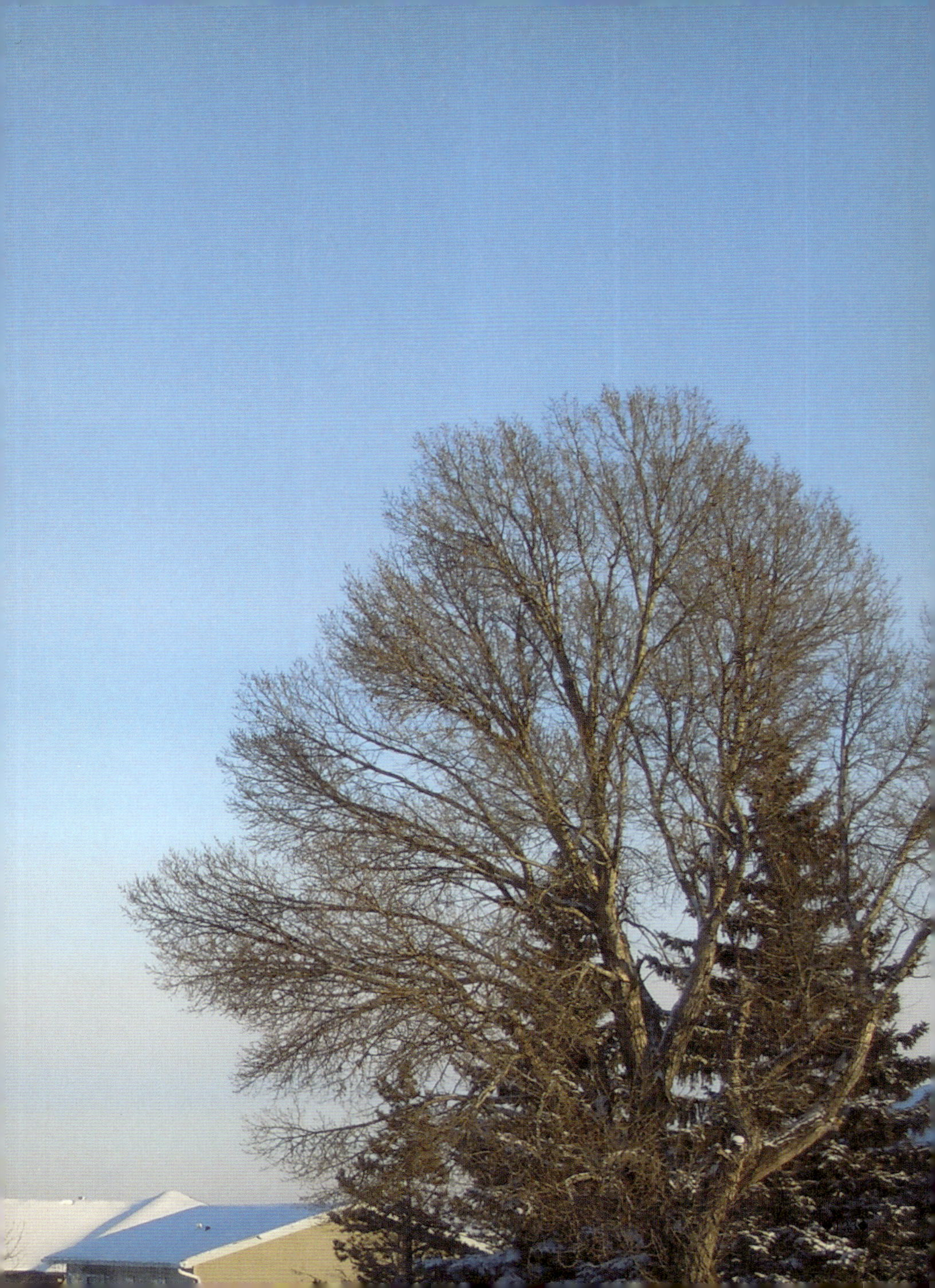

Chapter 9

◆

祈り

◆

Prayers

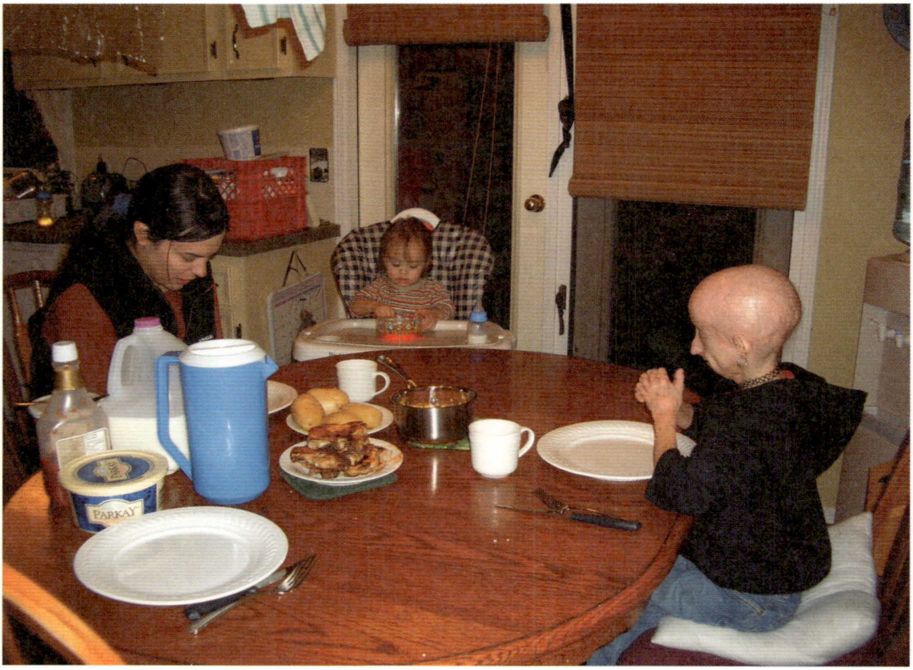
PARKAY

朝昼晩のお食事の前と寝る前の最低4回は、
お祈りをするわね。
ときには、もっとすることもある。

Before my breakfast, lunch, supper, and bedtime,
at least four times a day, I pray to God.
Sometimes, I pray more than that.

眠れないときに、
窓辺でお祈りをすることもあるのよ。
空に向かってお祈りをすると、
ちょっと神様に近づいているような気がする。

When I can't sleep, I pray by the window.
When I pray facing the sky,
I feel a little bit closer to God.

神様はきっと、すごく大きい人だと思う。
だって、彼は世界中の人たちのことを見ているんだもの。

あまりにスゴすぎて、想像することもできない。
もし絵を描いてみて、と言われても、
描くことなんてできない。

わたしたちの祈っていることに対して、
神様がそうしたいとお思いになったときは、
必ずかなえてくださるんだと思っているわ。

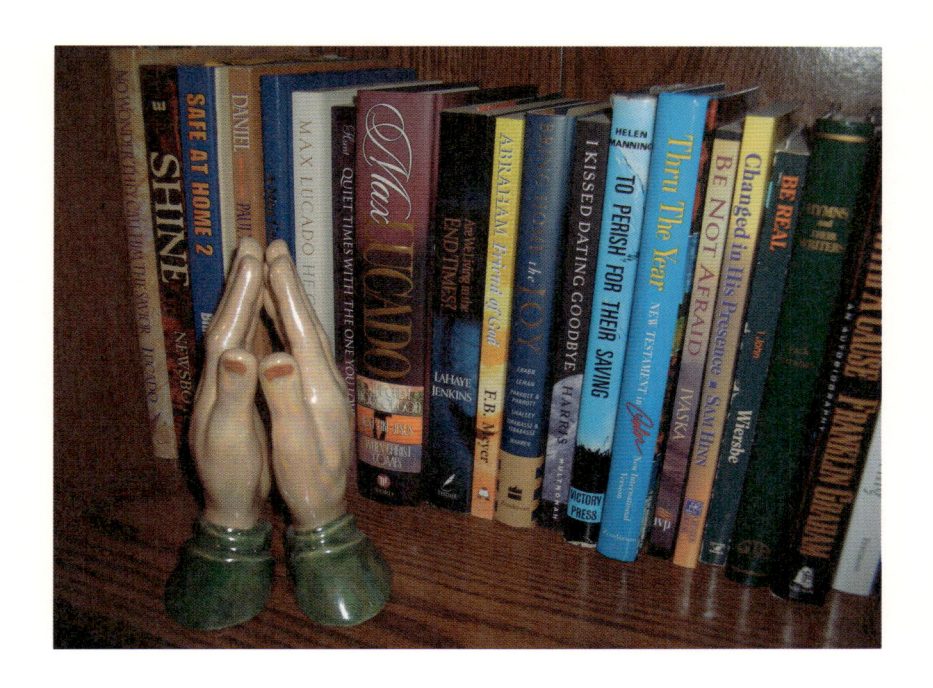

I think God is very, very big.
He is looking at everyone around the world at the same time,
so He must be very big.

God is so great that
I can't even imagine what He looks like.
If someone asked me to draw a picture of him, I couldn't do it.

I believe our wishes will come true
when God decides to make them happen...

天国は、いろんな色があるところだと思う。
この世で見たこともない色にあふれている
カラフルな場所だと思う。
滝があって、
豪邸だったりするんじゃない？
そして、暖かいところで、
誰一人悲しむこともなく、
泣くことも怒ることも
けっしてない。
みんな、いつも幸せなの。

I think there would be a lot of different colors in Heaven.
It would be so colorful,
and some colors would be like we've never seen in this world.
Maybe there would be waterfalls and mansions.
It would be warm,
and no one would feel sad there.
No one there would need to cry or get angry, either.
Everyone would always be happy in Heaven.

LOVE IS PATIENT LOVE IS KIND IT DOES NOT ENVY IT DOES NOT BOAST IT IS NOT PROUD IT IS NOT RUDE IT IS NOT SELF-SEEKING IT IS NOT EASILY ANGERED IT KEEPS NO RECORD OF WRONGS LOVE DOES NOT DELIGHT IN EVIL BUT REJOICES WITH THE TRUTH IT ALWAYS PROTECTS ALWAYS TRUSTS ALWAYS HOPES ALWAYS PERSEVERES LOVE NEVER FAILS AND NOW THESE THREE REMAIN FAITH HOPE AND LOVE BUT THE GREATEST OF THESE IS LOVE

わたしの人生に感謝します。
家族の健康と安全に感謝します。
今日一日無事に過ごせて感謝します。
そして、いい休息がもてますように。
家族が無事でありますように。
ひどい頭痛や胸の痛みが起こりませんように。
関節炎が痛みませんように。
明日も学校でいい一日が過ごせますように。
明日の朝、リフレッシュした気持ちで
起きられますように——。

I thank God for my life.
I thank God for keeping my family safe and healthy.
I thank God that I spent my day in safety.
I thank God for not having any chest pain, headache, or arthritis pain.
I pray that my family will be safe, and I will have a nice day in school tomorrow.
I pray that I will have a good night's rest,
and wake up tomorrow feeling refreshed...

Chapter 10

◆

夢

◆

Dreams

子どものころは、

獣医さんになりたいと思っていた。

ロックスターになりたいと思っていた。

パパがほしかった。

弟か妹がほしかった。

小さいころの夢はたくさんあったわ。

When I was little...
I always wanted to be a vet.
I always wanted to be a rock star.
I always wanted to have another dad.
I always wanted to have a brother or sister.
I had a whole bunch of dreams.

いまは、特別な夢ってないの。

家族がずっとずっと健康で

幸せでいてくれたら、それでいい。

Now I don't really have any particular dream,
as long as my family will have a long, happy, healthy life.
That's really about it

自分がいま得ているもので十分幸せだと思うから、

それ以上、ほかに思いつかないわ。

I'm happy with what I've got,
so I can't think of anything else.

夢というほどおおげさなものじゃないけど、
できたら絵本を作れたらいいなあ、と思っているの。

7年生のときに、
お話を書くという課題が出されたことがあって、
そのときはじめてお話を書いたの。
書いてみたら、とっても面白くて、
それ以来、お話を書くのが趣味になったの。

時間があるときに、
ひらめいたお話を書いているのよ。
あとで、あれを加えたらいいかなって思うこともあって、
思いついては書き加えたりしているの。

I sometimes think it would be nice if I could publish a picture book.

When I was in grade seven, we had to write a story in class.
That was the first story I wrote.
I started to like writing stories and since then it has kind of become my hobby.

Whenever I have time, I just jot down a few words.
Later, I'll think, "oh, I should put this into the story," and go back and write it down.

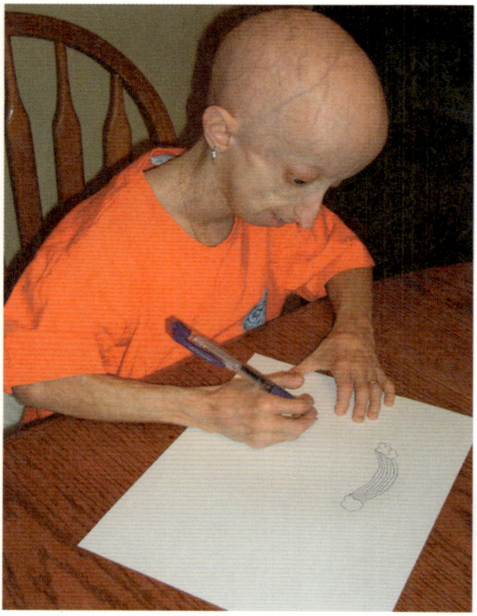

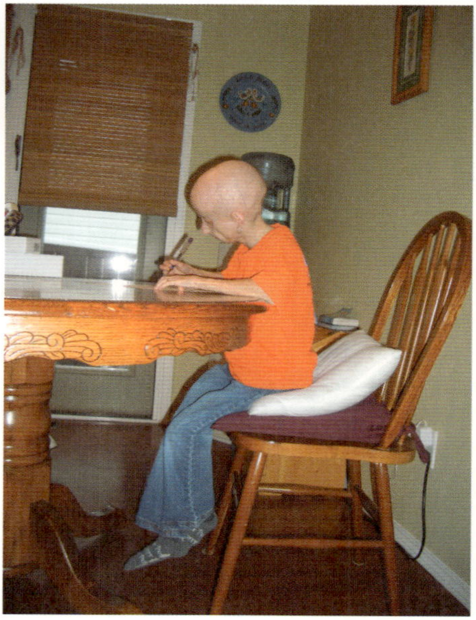

もともと絵を描くのは好きだったの。
物心ついたころから、
ひまなときにはよく絵を描いていたの。
家族にプレゼントするカードも、
絵を描いて手作りするのよ。
絵が好きに生まれついたって感じね。

たまには、こんな絵を描いたらいいかなって、
書きあげたお話に絵をつけることもあるのよ。

Ever since I was little, I've liked to draw.
I draw pictures whenever I feel like it.
When I give cards to my family members,
I always draw pictures on them.
I think I was just born that way.

Sometimes I come up with an idea
for a drawing for my new story.

「秘密のカギ」っていうお話は、
課題で提出して先生にもほめられたのよ。
登場人物は、男の子と女の子、そしてイヌとネコ。
彼らがキャンプに行って、秘密の箱を見つけるの。
そのなかには、カギと紙切れが入っていて、
紙切れには「エンジェルがキスする」とあるの。
どういう意味なのか、さっぱりわからないんだけど、
二人は、とにかく宝探しをはじめるの。
キャンプをはったそばには美しい滝があって、
近くまで探検に行ったところで、男の子が
「なんて書いてあったっけ？」って女の子に聞くの。
で、女の子が「エンジェルがキスする、よ」って言うと、
突然、滝が流れを止めるの。呪文の言葉だったわけ。
現れたドアにカギを差し込むと、ドアが開いて、
二人は豪邸みたいにステキな場所を発見するの。
滝の奥の洞窟はドリームケイブだったのよ。
そして、二人と動物は幸せに暮らしましたっていうお話。
みんな、わたしのアイデアなのよ。
想像で書いたの。

I wrote a story called "The Secret Key."
It was a school assignment and the teacher praised me for my story.
There are a boy, a girl, a dog, and a cat in the story.
They all go camping together and find a secret box in a field.
In the box, they discover a key and a piece of paper that says, "angel's kisses."
They don't know what it means but decide to start a treasure hunt.
There is a beautiful waterfall near their camp and they go over to look at it.
The boy asks the girl what the piece of paper says.
The girl answers, "angel's kisses."
Suddenly the water stops and there is a door behind the waterfall.
The words are a spell!
So they try the key in the door and it opens.
Inside the door, they find a dreamlike cave like a wonderful mansion.
So they stay there with their dog and cat, and live happily ever after.
This story is my own idea. I wrote it all from my imagination.

最近チャレンジしているのは、

弟をハッピーにすること。

彼の面倒をみることにトライしているの。

One of my recent challenges is to make my little brother happy.
I've been trying to take good care of my brother.

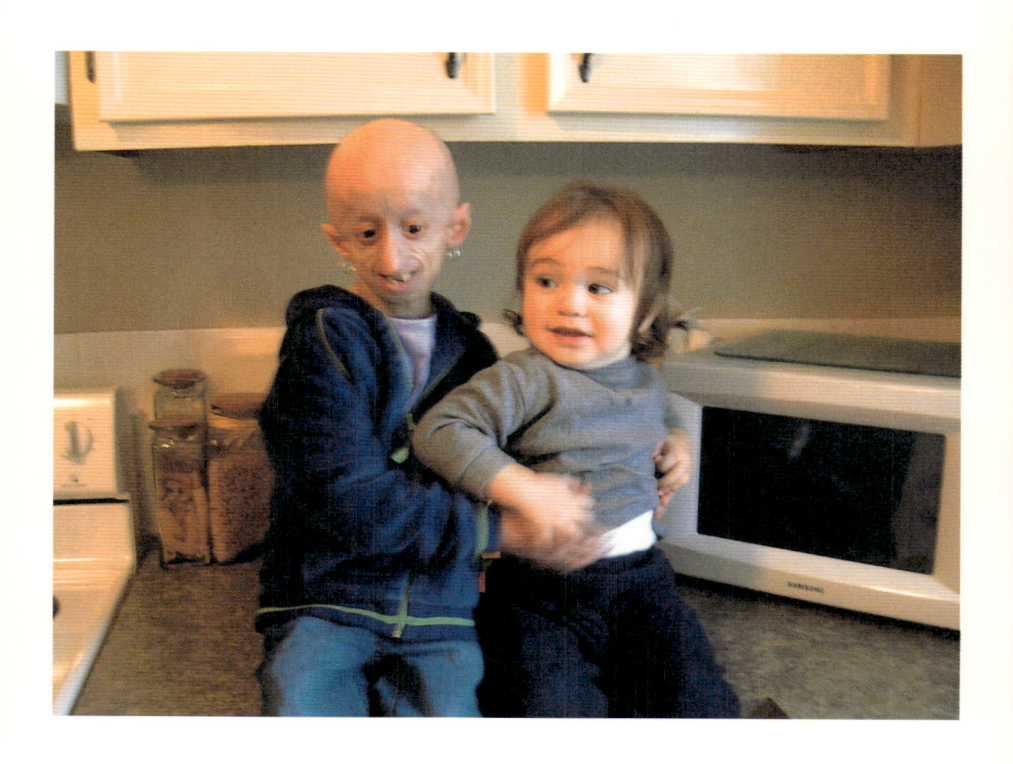

怒らないようにすることも、チャレンジね。

人に対して怒ったりしないようにしようって

決めたことは前に話したでしょ？

それはいまでも、ちゃんと続いているわよ。

I've also been trying not to get upset with others.
Like I told you before,
I decided not to get upset too easily.
It's been working so far.

ホントはね、熱帯雨林に行ってみたいの。
暑いところは平気。
ヘビがいたって平気よ。
雨もいっぱい降るけど、わたし、雨が好きなの。
水が落ちる音が好き。
雨はわたしをハッピーな気分にさせてくれるの。
それに、熱帯雨林には緑がいっぱいあって、
色とりどりの色彩にあふれているんでしょ？
わたし、それを見てみたいの。

でも、そのためには、
たくさん予防注射をしなければいけないじゃない？
わたしね、注射が大キライなのよ。
だから、まだトライしていないの。

I'd like to go to the rain forest.
I'd be fine with a place where it gets really hot.
I'd be fine with snakes, too.
The rain forest should rain a lot.
I like rain.
I like the sound of water falling.
Actually the rain makes me feel happy.
There would be a lot of greens and all those colors in the rain forest.
It'd be really neat if I could see them.

But, I would have to get many shots if I decided to go there.
I hate needles.
That's why I haven't even tried to go.

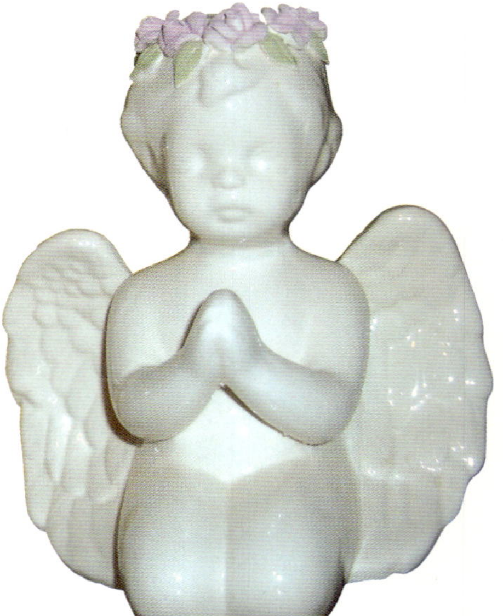

これからどうなりたいかって？
ハッピーで、みんなを勇気づける人になりたい。
人の助けになれる人になりたい。
愛情にあふれた人になりたい。

What would I like to be?
I'd like to be a happy and encouraging person.
I'd like to be a person who helps others.
I'd like to be a very loving person.

Chapter11

♦

ありがとう

♦

Thank You

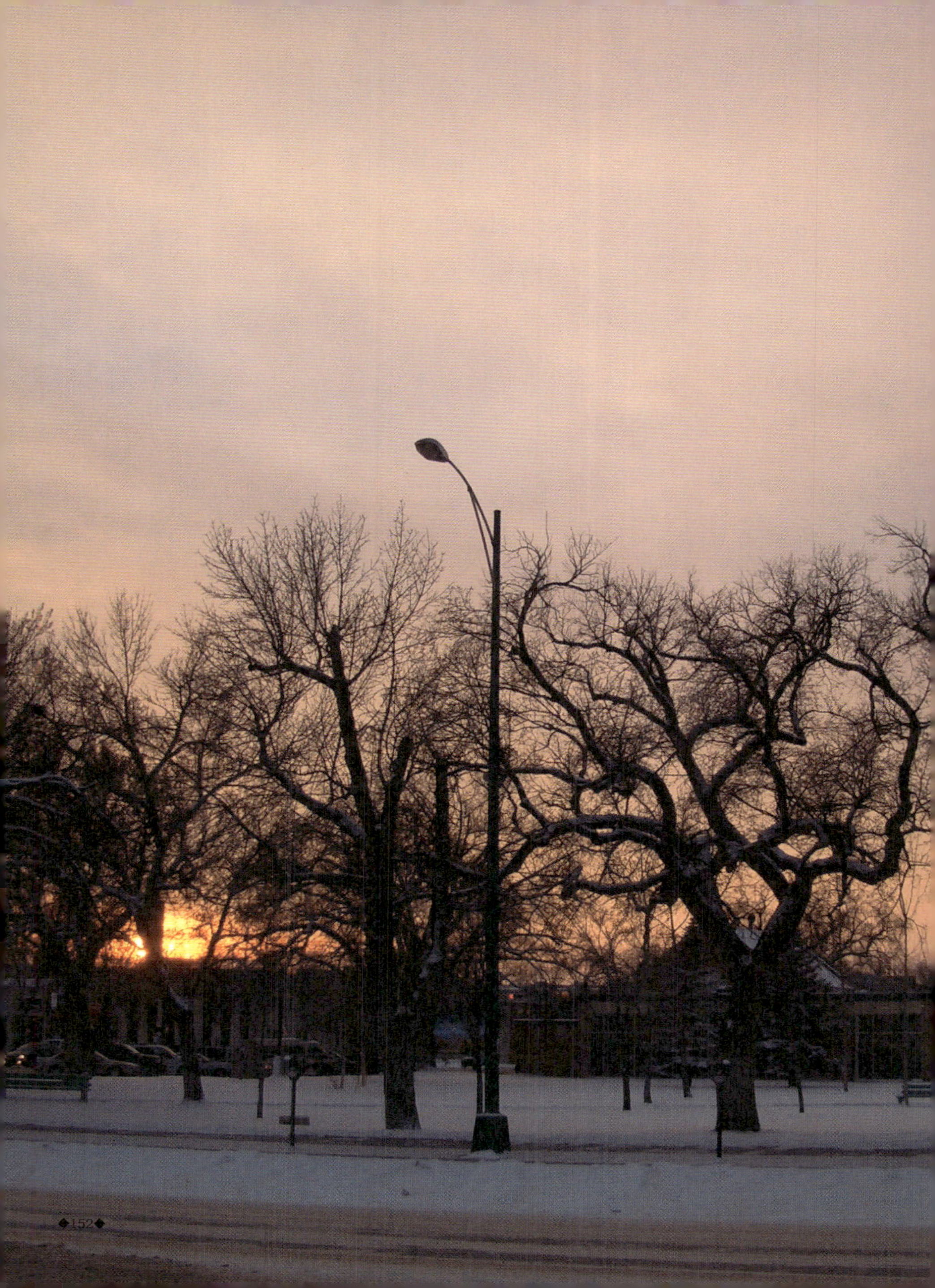

ふつうの人は、学校の友だちとか、
それ以外の友だちも、限られた範囲じゃない？
でも、わたしには世界中に友だちがいる。
たくさんの人が、会ったこともないのに、
わたしのことを知ってくれていて、
わたしと友だちになりたいって思ってくれている。

世界中のいろんなところに
わたしのことを知っている人がいるなんて、
とってもステキって感じ。

もしもいつか、みんなと会うことができたら、
すごくステキだな。

When someone says she has friends,
usually they are in the same school, or they are neighbors.
But I have a lot of friends around the world.
Many people whom I haven't even met yet know about me,
and they would like to be friends with me.

It is so nice that so many people
who live in different countries know about me.

If I could meet everyone, it would be neat.

テレビのドキュメンタリーを見たといって
日本からもたくさんお手紙をもらうのよ。

わたしが自分の生活を見せていることがスゴイ、
前向きな姿勢がスゴイって
みんな、言ってくれるの。
ときには、「こういう問題を抱えているんだけど、
どうすればいいと思う？」って
相談されることもあるの。

プレゼントもたくさんもらうの。
みんな大切にしているわ。
どれもうれしかったけど、いちばんうれしいのは、
「アイ・ラブ・ユー」っていう言葉。
これが、最高のプレゼントね。

I got a lot of letters from people
who watched my documentaries on TV in Japan.

They said it was inspiring that
I showed how I live and my attitude about life.
Sometimes people asked me, like,
" I have such and such problem so what should I do? "

I received many gifts from people in Japan and I cherish them all.
All of them were very nice.
The best gift I received was that people wrote me,
" I love you! "
It made me so happy.

いただいたお手紙にお返事はできないけれど、
もし書くんだったら、こう書くわ。
「プレゼントやお手紙をありがとう。
　わたしもお友だちになりたいわ。」

わたしは、みんなにも元気に前向きでいてほしいの。
わたしがわたしらしくいることで、
人を勇気づけることができているなら、
それは、とってもステキなことだと思うわ。

I wish I could write back to all the people who sent me letters.
If I could write back, I would say,
" I'd like to be friends with you, too."

I'd like everyone to be healthy and positive.
It's so nice to think that
I have encouraged people just by being myself.

Thanks for the things that have been sent
I appreciate it

ありがとう！

みんなもハッピーな笑顔でいてね。

Thank you so much, everyone!
Please be happy, and keep smiling!

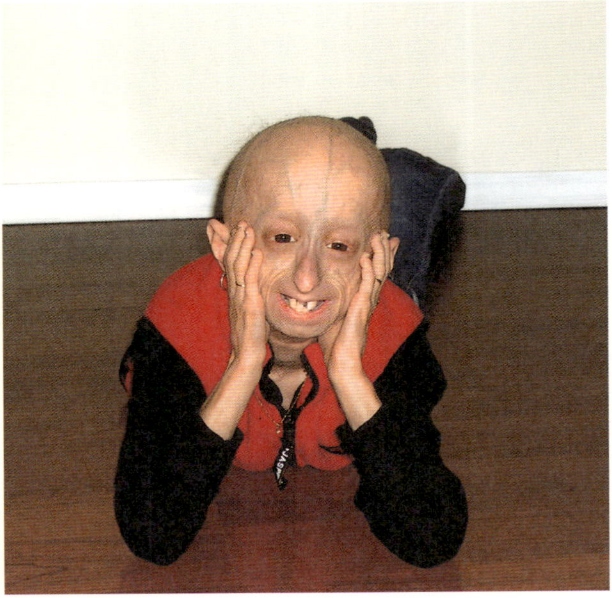

【番組スタッフ】

『サイエンスミステリー　それは運命か奇跡か!?
〜ＤＮＡが解き明かす人間の真実と愛〜』
第4章「短い命を刻む少女・アシュリー」

プロデューサー： 岡田宏記
岡島政利
ディレクター： 宮下佐紀子
加納丈嗣

【出版スタッフ】

ことば・イラスト・描き文字： アシュリー・ヘギ
構成・日本語テキスト・撮影： 伊東ひとみ
コーディネート・英語テキスト： 村山みちよ
装丁・本文デザイン： 小室杏子
編集担当： 草彅佐知子（扶桑社）

Love from Ashley

アシュリー ～All About Ashley～

2006年2月20日　　初版第1刷発行
2007年2月28日　　　　第7刷発行

著者： アシュリー・ヘギ
発行人： 山田良明
発行所： 株式会社フジテレビ出版
発売： 株式会社扶桑社
〒105-8070　東京都港区海岸1－15－1
TEL.03-5403-8859（販売）
TEL.03-5403-8870（編集）
http://www.fusosha.co.jp

印刷・製本： 図書印刷株式会社

定価はカバーに表示してあります。
落丁・乱丁（本の頁の抜け落ちや順序の間違い）の場合は
扶桑社販売部宛にお送りください。
送料は小社負担にてお取り替えいたします。

ISBN4-594-05114-6
© 2006 Ashley Hegi　Lori Ronald/Fuji Television Publishing,Inc.,
Printed in Japan